Rave Reviews!

"HIGH VOLTAGE SCORES WITH NEW *DRACULA!*"

"Dracula lives! Lugosi was the first to take it to the stage. 90 years later, the new [Christofer Cook and Dacre Stoker's] *Dracula* adaptation runs on stage through October. The big night will be on Halloween in West Columbia at the High Voltage Theatre!"

- Aaron Sagers,
Travel Channel

"When it comes to theatre, Cook isn't afraid to stare into the abyss, adapting and producing works of horror for the stage... It is as much a celebration of Bram Stoker's life as it is [a celebration of] the novel."

- Alison Lang
Rue Morgue

"Christofer Cook and Dacre Stoker, great-grand-nephew of Bram, have infused fresh life into a 19th-century classic; in doing so, they have created a viable stage *Dracula* for the new millennium, remaining true to the source novel while exploring unique dramatic territory suggested by live (or undead) performance."

- Meredith Merridew
The Free Times

DRACULA
OF TRANSYLVANIA

The Epic Play in Three Acts

Adapted from Bram Stoker's Novel by

CHRISTOFER COOK

Advisement to the Script by

DACRE STOKER

authorHOUSE®

AuthorHouse™
1663 Liberty Drive
Bloomington, IN 47403
www.authorhouse.com
Phone: 1 (800) 839-8640

Published by Authorhouse 05/26/2017,
World Dracula Day

ISBN: 978-1-4918-0878-8 (sc)
ISBN: 978-1-4918-0877-1 (e)

Christofer Cook

Titles

PROCLAMATION
of Association

Whereas, the first Stoker Family-endorsed, scripted stage-adaptation of Bram Stoker's novel, DRACULA was granted by Florence Balcombe to theatrical producer, Hamilton Deane in 1924, subsequently entitled *DRACULA, The Vampire Play...*

Whereas, *Dracula, the Vampire Play*, premiered on Broadway in 1927 (Produced by Horace Liveright and starring Bela Lugosi in the title role) and was considered the first produced, and published dramatization for the stage under consent and cooperation of Florence Balcombe, then custodian of Bram Stoker's estate,....

Be It Known that

DRACULA,
of Transylvania
Adapted by Christofer Cook & Advised by Dacre Stoker

Is Recognized As; the first stage adaptation of Bram Stoker's novel, DRACULA, adapted as a play, into typed script, under the temporary collaboration and cooperation of the Bram Stoker Estate and the Stoker family, since 1927's *Dracula, the Vampire Play.*

Is Recognized As; the first stage adaptation of Bram Stoker's DRACULA to be performed under the temporary collaboration and cooperation of the Bram Stoker Estate and the Stoker family since 1927, when Bela Lugosi played the title role on Broadway.

Is Recognized As; the first stage adaptation of Bram Stoker's DRACULA to be published with advisement to the script by a member of the Stoker family, since Florence Balcombe's association with Horace Liveright in 1927.

Thus saith all, in witness thereof;
Christofer Cook, Dramatists' Guild of America

CAUTION

Professionals and amateurs are hereby warned that *DRACULA of Transylvania* by Christofer Cook and Advised by Dacre Stoker, is subject to a royalty. It is fully protected under the copyright laws of the United States of America, and of all countries covered by the International Copyright Union (Including the Dominion of Canada and the rest of the British Commonwealth), and of all countries covered by the Pan-American Copyright Convention and the Universal Copyright Convention, and of all countries with which the United States has reciprocal copyright relations. All rights, including professional, amateur, motion picture, recitation, lecturing, public reading, radio broadcasting, television, video or sound taping, all other forms of mechanical or electronic reproduction, such as information storage, retrieval systems and photocopying, downloading, streaming video, and the rights of translation into foreign languages are strictly reserved. Particular emphasis is laid upon the question of readings, permission and terms for which must be secured from the author in writing.

The stage performance rights for *DRACULA of Transylvania* by Christofer Cook, Advised by Dacre Stoker, are controlled exclusively by the playwright. No professional or non-professional performance of the play may be given without obtaining in advance the written permission of the dramatist and paying the requisite royalty fees. All inquiries concerning rights to the play should be addressed to;

Christofer Cook
HighVoltageSC@aol.com
(803) 429-8839.

1625 Malcolm Drive
Columbia, SC 29204

SPECIAL NOTE

Anyone receiving permission to produce *DRACULA of Transylvania*, A Play in Three Acts by Christofer Cook, advised by Dacre Stoker, is subject to the following proviso: Producing theatres, schools, and any and all other community groups, are required to give due authorship credit to the playwright as the sole and exclusive author of the play as well as due credit to Dacre Stoker as the sole and exclusive advisor to the script. The by-line should read 'Adapted from Bram Stoker's Novel by Christofer Cook' and then 'with Dacre Stoker, Script Advisor' just beneath. This must appear on all posters, websites, social-media advertising, programs, flyers, and any and all other promotional printing in connection with productions of the play. In all instances in which the title of the play appears for purposes of advertising, publicizing, or otherwise exploiting the play and/or a production thereof; the names of the playwright and advisor must appear on separate lines, in which no other name appears, immediately beneath the title and in size of type equal to 50% of the largest letter used for the title of the play. No person, firm, nor entity may receive credit larger than that accorded the playwright and advisor.

WELCOME TO COLUMBIA'S (OTHER) THEATER SCENE

Small Companies, DIY Ethic Expand Local Offerings

By August Krickel
Feature: *Free Times*
August 21, 2013

"Town Theatre produced plays nearly a century ago in an old house near the University of South Carolina campus, and Workshop Theatre began in borrowed auditoriums and vacant commercial space. Trustus Theatre started in a former punk rock club. That spirit of do-it-yourself ambition thrives today in a number of newer theatrical groups, which might not sell the number of tickets that the larger groups do, but nevertheless show the same drive.

Christofer Cook led the way in 2002 with High Voltage Theatre, 'a professional theatre [i.e., the performers are paid] enhanced by our community.' Returning to his native Columbia armed with an Master of Fine Arts degree in directing and more than a decade of professional experience in big cities like New York and Chicago, Cook pitched the idea of a live Halloween production of *The Legend of Sleepy Hollow* to students at Midlands Technical College while serving as an adjunct faculty member, and his company was born. A rusted sign on a power grid reading 'Danger! High Voltage!' suggested the group's name.

'We were young, new, exciting,' he recalls. 'We would venture out into more raw and edgy, dangerous theatre.' Cook penned the original script, and *Sleepy Hollow* has been a popular Halloween attraction ever since, most often performed at the West Columbia Riverwalk Amphitheater, and usually the top-selling live theater show running locally during October. Other productions have included adaptations of *Reservoir Dogs, Phantom of the Opera,* and *A Night of the Living Dead.* Cook is particularly proud of a 'Woodstock moment' when more than 350 people showed up for the 200 seats available for *Sleepy Hollow* in 2004.

While he once considered a permanent facility, he is now 'happy not having to pay rent on a performance space. West Columbia donates the amphitheater to us because we bring in capital and raise their hospitality numbers. And I'm comfy with that.' Cook does stage combat workshops in schools, as well as gigs as a magician and fight choreographer, but High Voltage is his primary focus. A number of his plays are now available in book form, and his adaptation of *Sleepy Hollow* has been performed across the country.

The next High Voltage project is a collaboration with Dacre Stoker, great grand-nephew of Bram Stoker for the world premiere of *The Bram Stoker Estate Dracula*, opening October 10th and running through Halloween at the West Columbia Riverwalk Amphitheater."

JASPER FANCIES: BLOOD!

By Gus Hart
Feature: *Jasper Magazine*
Sept / Oct, 2013

"Christofer Cook fell under the spell of *Dracula* when he played Renfield, the Count's mad, insect-eating minion, in an A.C. Flora High School production, with a young Kristin Davis (*Sex & the City, Melrose Place*) as heroine Lucy. The lifelong fan of the horror genre and founder of High Voltage Theatre is now collaborating with Dacre Stoker; great-grand nephew of *Dracula* author Bram Stoker; to bring the world premiere of *DRACULA of Transylvania* to the West Columbia Riverwalk Amphitheatre, just in time for Halloween.

After studying playwriting with Pulitzer-Prize winner Beth Henley and earning an MFA in Directing at Chicago's Roosevelt University, Cook felt ready in 2002 to lead his own professional company, emulating the itinerant structure of the SC Shakespeare Company where he had both acted and directed. The name High Voltage would signify a more aggressive, gritty, in-your-face style of performance often incorporating Cook's skills as a stage magician and fight choreographer. Early productions at assorted venues included edgy fare like *Reservoir Dogs* and *Cowboy Mouth*, but Cook's original adaptation of *The Legend of Sleepy Hollow* was a perennial crowd-pleaser, and the group's mission evolved to focus on horror and the macabre. Recent shows have included *A Night of the Living Dead* at Tapp's, *Phantom of the Opera* at the Riverwalk Amphitheater, and *Frankenstein*, performed live at the Civil War – era historical dock at Granby Locks in 2009, with future mayoral candidate Aaron Johnson in the title role and Cook as the Creature.

Cook directs his own adaptations of these classic stories, and a number of his scripts are now available in book form; in addition to its seven incarnations locally, *Sleepy Hollow* is performed several times a year by professional and amateur groups across the country.

While planning for *DRACULA of Transylvania* earlier this year, Cook discovered that Dacre Stoker, co-author of *Dracula: The Undead*, an "official" 2009 sequel to the original 1897 novel, lived in Aiken, South Carolina. "I'd be a fool not to try to reach out to him," Cook recalls, hoping to enlist Stoker's help as a creative consultant, or at least receive his blessing. What started as an informal chat over coffee quickly developed into a full-fledged collaboration between High Voltage and the Bram Stoker Estate.

Dacre Stoker, a native of Montreal and a Pentathlon champion who coached the Canadian Pentathlon team in the 1988 Summer Olympics, currently works as a tennis professional, and has become the Stoker family historian. In addition to his first novel, he has developed a multi-media lecture show, "Stoker on Stoker", produced a documentary about his ancestor, and co-authored the non-fiction *Bram Stoker's Lost Journal*.

Kindred spirits, he and Cook shared a desire to return the story to its roots in the theatre. For nearly 30 years, Bram Stoker's day job was business manager of Sir Henry Irving's Lyceum Theatre in London. Irving's commanding presence may have influenced Stoker's depiction of Dracula's hold over Renfield, while Irving's portrayal of Iachimo in *Cymbeline*, a villain who lies concealed in a coffin-like chest before emerging to menace the sleeping heroine by night, has more than a few echoes of Stoker's novel, published the very next year. Stoker wrote a stage version, which received a reading at the Lyceum, but Irving never played the lead in an actual production.

Decades later Hamilton Deane wrote a new adaptation which was significantly re-written by John L. Balderston for Broadway, where Bela Lugosi found fame in the lead. That variation, drastically different from the novel, is the source of most modern versions. Cook and Dacre Stoker have added a framing device, based on "the Icelandic Preface," a later introduction penned by Bram Stoker in which he declares the events detailed herein are all true. While clearly the literary equivalent of "names have been changed to protect the innocent," Cook feels that Stoker was also drawing on contemporary fears in a London where women and children regularly went missing, and the Jack the Ripper murders were a recent memory.

"Dacre and I have a creative synergy," Cook says, "bouncing ideas off each other. I'm the one with my fingers on the keyboard, while he's the one pacing the room." Cook is also fond of the British comedies of manners of Noel Coward and Oscar Wilde, and promises a few laughs amidst the mayhem. He signs off in correspondence with "Bloody Best," and early press material for the production is sent with the title "Scary Stuff!"

He notes that this is the first stage adaptation since the 1927 Deane-Balderston treatment to receive official authorization and endorsement by the Bram Stoker Estate. The title role will be played by Alfred Kern, recently seen as Mr. Bennett in *Pride and Prejudice* at Finlay Park, while Cook will play Renfield. *DRACULA of Transylvania* opens Thursday, October 17, and runs through Halloween at the West Columbia Riverwalk Amphitheater. A website, DraculaPlay.com, will soon go live, while information on High Voltage Theatre can be found via Facebook."

BRAM STOKER ESTATE *
ENDORSES NEW THEATRICAL
PRODUCTION OF DRACULA

By Alison Lang
Feature: *Rue Morgue Magazine*
Halloween Issue / Oct, 2013

"When it comes to theatre, Christofer Cook isn't afraid to stare into the abyss – and make it family-friendly. For the past thirteen years, the South Carolina-based artistic director of High Voltage Theatre has dedicated himself to adapting and producing works of classic horror for the stage, geared towards audiences of all ages.

After mounting popular productions of *The Legend of Sleepy Hollow, Phantom of the Opera,* and *A Night of the Living Dead*, Cook decided he wanted to tackle one of the most classic gothic tales of all time, *Dracula* - and on a whim, he thought he might try reaching out to one of Bram Stoker's descendants, his great, grand nephew Dacre Stoker. Stoker is considered an authority on his famous ancestor and the historical context surrounding the novel, and vampire fans may recall that in 2009, he co-authored a sequel to *Dracula* titled *Dracula: The Undead*.

"I'd read the sequel and loved it," says Cook. "I wondered if he might be interested in hearing about my adaptation and maybe even coming to see it."

Cook discovered that the Canadian-born Stoker was living in Aiken, South Carolina – an hour – and – a - half drive from Columbia. He reached out to the author/historian through Facebook and met him in person soon afterwards. They hit it off, and were soon getting together frequently to discuss the play and its details.

"I realized we were becoming collaborators, and Dacre was becoming my co-author on this project,' says Cook. The relationship proved to be reciprocal: Cook's writing benefited from Stoker's knowledge of his great grand – uncle and the novel, while Stoker relished the opportunity to learn more about playwriting. Additionally, Stoker took the initiative to submit the play to the Bram Stoker Estate, maintained by a group of his cousins, to see if they'd authenticate and endorse it. They did, and the play was retitled *The Bram Stoker Estate Dracula*. It's the first stage production that has received this endorsement since 1927, when Bela Lugosi played the title role.

'I've done a lot of research on how difficult it was for everyone to adapt *Dracula* onto the stage – there have been hundreds of versions,' Stoker says. 'At first I wasn't writing much of the dialogue with Chris, but as my confidence grew, he wanted ideas of what should and shouldn't go into the play.' One major addition is the incorporation of a special preface that has only ever appeared in a 1901 Icelandic translation of the novel. In it, Stoker addresses the reader directly, writing that everything they are about to read is true. Both Cook and Stoker found this irresistible, and rewrote the preface as a framing monologue addressing the audience, where Stoker himself becomes a pivotal character, gradually revealing the 'truth' to the audience. 'As far as we know, no one has done anything like this before dramatically,' Cook notes. 'This is as much a celebration of Bram Stoker's life as it is [a celebration] of the novel.'

For Stoker, the inclusion of his ancestor as a character has evolved into an opportunity to delve even further into his family's ancestry. 'Bram Stoker was a 'noticer', he explains. 'He was aware of everything and the world around him and he was willing to make a difference with those issues and he did. He was concerned with socialism, health, science and technology; his mother was a social activist, he was a civil servant and wanted to adjust the law. This play is a chance to show people a side of Bram that they may not have been previously familiar with.'

Stoker and Cook say they will be sticking closely to the original storyline, with the preface serving as the only major addition. 'It's just [fresh] enough to cast a shadow of doubt and make people a little uneasy,' says Stoker. 'This is something I love about horror – those things that make you feel a little uneasy about the world around you.' *The Bram Stoker Estate Dracula* runs from October 17 to October 31 at the Outdoor Riverwalk Amphitheater in West Columbia, South Carolina. More information available at DraculaPlay.com."

HIGH VOLTAGE SCORES WITH NEW DRACULA

Production Runs Through Oct 31 at Riverwalk Amphitheater

By Meredith Merridew
Theatre Review: *Free Times*
Friday, October 25th, 2013

"All it takes is new blood. Christofer Cook, founder of High Voltage Theatre and Dacre Stoker, great-grand-nephew of Bram, have infused new life into a 19th- Century classic; in doing so, they have created a viable stage Dracula for the new millennium, remaining true to the source novel while exploring new dramatic territory suggested by live (or undead?) performance. The world premiere of *DRACULA of Transylvania* endorsed by and developed in collaboration with the Bram Stoker Estate is quite a coup for Columbia, or more accurately West Columbia, where the Count will be menacing maidens and sucking blood in the Riverwalk Amphitheater through Thursday, October 31.

Bram Stoker's 1897 plot, often altered or discarded entirely in stage and screen adaptations, is followed closely. Young lawyer Jonathan travels to Transylvania (rural mountainous Romania) to work on real estate contracts for the reclusive Count. After 400 years in isolation in the Balkan equivalent of West Virginia, Dracula craves a change of venue to merry old England. Scenes of Jonathan's growing realization of his host's true nature alternate with London vignettes of his sensible fiancé Mina indulging in Jane Austen-style banter with her giddy cousin Lucy.

Lucy is pursued by three suitors: brooding nobleman Arthur, dashing American cowboy Quincy, and dedicated physician Jack, who happens to run the neighboring "lunatic asylum". Before long, Lucy succumbs to some pernicious anemia, and Seward's mentor Professor Van Helsing is called in. Whereupon mayhem ensues.

Cook and Dacre Stoker are successful in three major areas: flowing language, expanded characterizations, and visual moments of eerie silence on stage. The novel is written as a series of letters, news articles, and diary and journal extracts, but here the author's sometimes turgid Victorian prose is melded seamlessly with new dialogue by the playwrights. The audience still understands that these are people speaking a more formalized type of English from long ago, but words are easily understood, including some complex sections of exposition about the vampire's nature. Dracula, Lucy, and mad minion Renfield all benefit from enhanced and extended speeches – practically soliloquies – that give their portrayers plenty of material to… well, to sink their teeth into, while fleshing out characters that are often depicted as little more than plot devices. It's still a very talky play with nods to the quips and bon mots of period wits like Shaw and Wilde, but then one or more vampires will silently enter from the hillside and woods that flank the performance space and the effect is genuinely chilling.

Alfred Kern as Dracula with his flat, methodical delivery and his long, flowing grey hair is reminiscent of Alan Rickman... until you realize that Alan Rickman would actually make an incredible Dracula, just a different one than traditionally portrayed. There's much more subtlety and nuance in Kern's Slavic monotone than is immediately apparent, and you realize that it's actually carefully underplayed restraint. The playwrights give him a terrific speech connecting to the historical Dracula, aka Vlad the Impaler, and Kern's hair, mustache and beard channel Vlad perfectly.

Cook makes no secret of his love for the Renfield character, whom he first played in high school. As Renfield, here Cook looks like Hell. Literally – he resembles Satan. His scarlet jumpsuit is actually long underwear, his leather and chains are simply asylum restraints, and that's just unkempt hair, not horns above his forehead. Cook, the actor, steals his scenes away from the rest of the cast, but nevertheless, Renfield is a sight to behold, alternating between a defiant Lear-like figure and a cringing Gollum. (I wouldn't be at all surprised if Tokien drew on Renfield, already an archetype long before he ever wrote The Hobbit.)

Stephanie Walden takes top acting honors as Lucy, artfully tracing her transition from silly, shallow society girl to creature of the night. A friend accurately noted that Lucy really doesn't hesitate too much in embracing the dark side, and indeed seems all too proficient when she becomes an evil seductress. As she describes to Mina the conflict and passion running through her veins, she speaks directly to the audience, and when she proclaims "I THIRST!", chills are guaranteed to run down your spine. And you may want to offer your own neck to her, as the actress is gorgeous, and her performance is commanding.

During the promotion for this play, Chad Forrister (Quincy) challenged me to give him a bad review some day, but he's not getting one here. As in the book, Quincy and Arthur (Alexis Casanovas) are underwritten; indeed the characters are often merged into one. I've always seen Quincy as a Texas gentleman, not a rip-roarin' "I'll be hornswoggled!" gunslinger, but the character here is written the way a Brit of Irish heritage would imagine an American to behave. Forrister, adept at broadly-drawn characters, is up for the challenge, and would make a great Wyatt Earp in some High Voltage play as-yet-unwritten. Casanovas has nice moments of restrained physicality as we watch Lucy essentially die in real time before us. Nathan Dawson as Jack is excellent, depicting a decent young man of science, although one a little too starchy and clinical to appeal to the lively Lucy.

Brittany Bierman does solid work as Mina, while William Cavitt has a baby face but a rich mature voice, both perfect for Jonathan. Cavitt stepped into the role only two weeks before opening, but completely carries his half of extended scenes with Dracula. David Reed as Van Helsing recalls the eccentric portrayal of Anthony Hopkins from the 1992 Coppola film; alone among the "gentlemen" he wears no necktie or cravat, a radical statement for that era. The playwrights accentuate his quirkiness for comic effect, but Reed manages to deliver plenty of lines with gravity and solemnity.

Laura Dixon, Breck Cronise, and Haley Claffy are slinky and menacing as the three vampire brides of Dracula; Claffy doubles as a London nurse who attends the dying Lucy, and you'd never know it was the same actress if not for her petite stature. That actually enhances the role, because one imagines that she was some young tween transformed by Dracula, who then became as sexy and predatory as her older, taller peers.

Costumes by Alice Perkins, sound design by Blanchard Williams (incorporating appropriate mood music at crucial moments, as well as realistic sounds of bats at windows, wolves howling in the distance, and a baby crying) and lighting by Rufus Carson (using floods of red at moments you'd expect) are all excellent. The set by West Jenkins, a menacing stone and mortar interior with assorted nooks, crannies, and portals is adequate. Actors are on the raised stage and the larger sandy gravel area in front is used where the performers have room to move around. Only area microphones are used, and the actors generally project better than any number of recent indoors shows I've seen, where performers sport head mikes and still can't be heard.

Use of stage magic and special effects are accomplished solely by the actors with no technology. There is one especially striking effect: it involves a sort of telekinetic push by Lucy, and later by Dracula, and the result is as good as anything on the big screen.

DRACULA of Transylvania is a decent and admirable first performance of a new adaptation of a hugely popular and influential work. Believe it or not, it's also relatively family-friendly. Blood is minimal, skin even less so, and there's more creepy suspense than actual horror. I first read the novel in a frenzied 24-hour marathon aided by a flashlight under the covers, shortly after the last day of 6th grade, and that seems about the right age to be able to first appreciate the material. While the theatrical performances of the cast and the script's language is reminiscent of Shakespeare, the overall tone is perhaps closest to the Hammer films of the late 1950's. Now, if you're going, be sure to bring some folding chairs or at least stadium cushions to sit on. Weather is tricky this time of year, so an extra jacket or blanket wouldn't be amiss, and perhaps an umbrella."

'DRACULA of Transylvania', Succeeds with High Stakes!

By August Krickel
Theatre Review: *Onstage Columbia*
Wednesday, October 23rd, 2013

Christofer Cook and Dacre Stoker, playwright and script advisor, respectively, have accomplished the oft-elusive objective of their contemporaries; fashioning a world-renown literary classic into a stage play that is both relevant and engaging for modern-day audiences. Their rich and intricately crafted script is that rarest of stage properties, a *Dracula* that offers a satisfying live alternative to decades of cinematic gore and computer-generated mayhem. The adaptors' respect for the source material retains Bram Stoker's florid, near-Shakespearean prose without sacrificing suspense, thrills, chills, or good old-fashioned action. This is the purest of portraits presented plein-air, staged in an outdoor amphitheater near the banks of a vast river. This allows for unexpected entrances and exits, and a sense of the foreboding grandeur of nature. This new adaptation incorporates all of the best fan-favorites: Harker's journey to and harrowing escape from Transylvania, the enticing and seductive brides of Dracula, Lucy's wasting illness, the heroic valor of her three suitors, confrontations with the "Bloofer Lady", and Dracula's gypsy minions. I was particularly pleased with an expanded acknowledgement of the Count's connection to the historical Prince Vlad, tragic defender of Wallachia and/or evil impaler of his enemies. The natural limitations of live performance are cleverly accommodated by the author's suggestions for staging, making *Dracula of Transylvania* an attractive choice for directors working within every budget, at every type of venue, and every level of theatre.

- A Disclaimer: The previews, reviews, and articles above were published during the early stages of a temporary partnership between the Bram Stoker Estate and High Voltage Theatre. However, this play is not officially endorsed by the Bram Stoker Estate. Rather, it is a verifiably-historical literary document resulting from a collaboration and association between playwright, Christofer Cook, and the Stoker family, descendents of Bram Stoker. No misrepresentation of *DRACULA of Transylvania* in relation to the Bram Stoker Estate is intended.

For

Dacre & Jenne Stoker,

of The Bram Stoker Estate

with eternal gratitude
for your generosity, patience,
inspiration, and encouragement
throughout the process.

DRACULA of Transylvania, a Play in Three Acts, is by Christofer Cook, with script advisement by Dacre Stoker. It made its world premiere on October 17th, of 2013. The show was produced by High Voltage Theatre and presented at the Riverwalk Amphitheater in West Columbia, South Carolina. The production was directed by Mr. Cook and advised by Mr. Stoker. The cast was as follows:

Count Dracula	Alfred Kern
Abraham Van Helsing	David Reed
Mina Murray	Brittany Bierman
Jonathan Harker	William Cavitt
Dr. Jack Seward	Nathan Dawson
Arthur Holmwood / Lord Godalming	Alexis Casanovas
Quincy P. Morris	Chadwick Forrester
Lucy Westenra	Stephanie Walden
R.M. Renfield	Christofer Cook
Mrs. Westenra / Patti Hennessey	Teresa McWilliams
Woman in White #1	Laura Dixon
Woman in White #2	Breck Cronise
Woman in White #3 / Smollet Snelling	Haley Claffy
Waites Simmons	Dillon Winter
Ian Paterson/ Coachman	John Dixon
Innkeeper's Wife / Mildred Creapley	Alice Perkins
Nigel Billington	Austin Gilbert
Mr. Swales / Train Conductor	Keats Rowell
Innkeeper / Gypsy Guard	Evan Franklin
Boy	Henry Dawson

Stage Manager was Blanchard Williams, Set design was by West Jenkins, Construction by West Jenkins and Roy Williamson. Costumes designed by Lydia Latham, Hilda Palacios, and Alice Perkins. Special Effects Make-Up by Courtney Slocumb. Lighting by Rufus Carson, Dance Choreography was by Tracy Steele.

THE USAGE OF 'WILL' VERSUS 'SHALL' IN THE SCRIPT

Much is made of the usage of 'will' and 'shall' with regard to drama. Contemporary plays won't likely use the word 'shall' at all. But being that this is a story set mostly in late 19th Century England, we felt that the use of 'shall' was rather fitting. Every effort has been made to adhere to the rules set forth by Oxford English. To make it simple, we have used 'shall' in first-person circumstances. This is allowed in both future emotional states of being; ie, "I shall go mad." as well as determined future events of physical action; ie "I shall travel the black sea". We have used 'will' in second and third-person circumstances; ie, "They will arrive shortly." and in commands such as "You will open Renfield's cell door immediately!" The script has been carefully culled to insure this consistency in usage. Any deviation from the above rule is unintentional and an oversight. In the end, what is important is clarity of ideas. Whether an actor says "shall" or "will" in a given circumstance should never yield any significant consequence to the story being told.

Sanguis enim eorum pro anima.

ACT I

Breakdown of Scenes

(10-Minute Intermission)

Scene 1

"The Golden Krone"

[Bistriz, Romania – 1893]

(At rise we see the exterior of the Golden Krone Hotel, Bistriz. 1893. There is low-lying fog creeping about, an azure blue by the light of the moon. Mysterious music of instrumental nature eases in with lights. Innkeeper's Wife, Innkeeper, and Jonathan Harker enter the scene in music. The Innkeeper carries Jonathan's suitcase, while Jonathan carries his own valise. They step out in front of the Hotel to wait for the arrival of a carriage. In spite of the hour, a few villagers gather and look on with curiosity.)

INNKEEPER'S WIFE

Herr Englishman, have you enjoyed your
stay at the Hotel Golden Krone?

HARKER

A delightful place. Thank you.

INNKEEPER

You have traveled a great distance, yes?
And still you have far to go?

HARKER

Well, my travels began in Munich on the first of April. And as
you know, I arrived in Bistriz last night. A shorter journey

awaits me now. The coach is to arrive soon, in order that I may reach my final destination before dawn.

INNKEEPER

And to where does your business take you?

HARKER

I will be traveling to Bukovina, and on through the Borgo Pass. Deeper into the foothills of the Carpathians and then upward to the higher peaks.

INNKEEPER

The Carpathians?

HARKER

Yes.

INNKEEPER'S WIFE

Where, in the Carpathians?

HARKER

To the Castle Dracula.

(The Innkeeper, wife, and villagers make the sign of the cross.)

INNKEEPER'S WIFE

Dracula?

HARKER

What do you know of Count Dracula?

INNKEEPER

We must go now, Sir.

HARKER

But, wait! Tell me,… What is it that disturbs you so?

INNKEEPER'S WIFE

We wish to speak no further. If you know what is good for you, you will turn 'round and go back from whence you came. Do you understand?

HARKER

But that's preposterous. My business with the Count is urgent.

INNKEEPER

Nothing, young man, is more urgent than preserving your life.

INKEEPER'S WIFE

Must you go? Oh Herr, must you go?

HARKER

Indeed. I must leave at once.

INNKEEPER

Do you know what day it is?

HARKER

It is the fourth of May.

INNKEEPER

Walpurgisnacht!

HARKER

I don't understand.

INNKEEPER'S WIFE

Walpurgisnacht. The eve of St. George's Day. Tonight, when the clock strikes midnight, all the evil things in the world will have full sway!

HARKER

My dear lady… Thank you for your concern, but I must go.

INNKEEPER'S WIFE

(On her knees.)

Please! Delay your trip for a few days!

(A horse approaches the main doorstep of the inn. It is pulling an open coach)

INNKEEPER
(To the Coachman.)

You are early tonight, my friend.

COACHMAN

We must make haste. Night will soon fall, and
midnight brings,… No, I shan't say.

INNKEEPER
(To the Coachman.)

Just as well. Our English Herr seems in a hurry.

COACHMAN
(To Harker.)

Fear not Sir. My horses are swift.

INNKEEPER

As in Burger's ballad, *Lenore*, I trust.
"Den die todten reiten schnell!"

COACHMAN
For the Dead travel Fast!

HARKER
I beg your pardon?

<u>INNKEEPER'S WIFE</u>

Here, Mine Herr. Take this. Wear it about your neck always. The crucifix of our savior. "For your mother's sake".

*(The old woman places a crucifix on a
rosary around Harker's neck.)*

<u>INNKEEPER</u>

It shall protect you in your travels. But, Mine Herr Harker, whatever you do,… Do not take it off.

<u>HARKER</u>

Thank you.

COACHMAN

Give me the Herr's baggage. We must make haste if we are to arrive at the Borgo Pass in good time. We must travel, we must travel, we must travel!

(Music in. Coachman and Harker exit.)

[END OF SCENE]

Scene 2

"A Garden Cemetery"

[Whitby, England]

(New, fresher music of delight and springtime eases in. Sunlight spilling in through trees warms the area; a garden alongside a cemetery at Whitby Cottage, a retreat for holiday owned by the Westenras. Enter Mina, Lucy, and Mrs. Westenra behind. Swales An old groundskeeper and gravedigger, enters carrying a valise belonging to Mina, in each hand. The young ladies, excited and holding hands, twirl about for a bit like a whirling dervish. Mrs. Westenra is happy to see the friends reunited once again. Swales sets the suitcases down, sits upon a bench for a moment, dabs his forehead with a cloth, then exits.)

<u>MINA</u>

We must travel together soon, Lucy!

<u>LUCY</u>

Mina, you must tell us all about your train ride through the moors.

<u>MINA</u>

There's nothing to tell, really. Just that I miss my Jonathan and so wish he could come spend this glorious holiday with us here at your cottage in Whitby. And, I have been looking forward to my time with you both.

LUCY

Trouble yourself not, Mina. Jonathan will be here soon enough.

MINA

I trust you will forgive my delays in writing but I have been simply overwhelmed with work. The life of an assistant schoolmistress is sometimes trying.

MRS. WESTENRA

Mina, Dear. Let me have a look at you. Yes, as beautiful as always! And how is that handsome solicitor of yours?

(Mina pulls out a few letters. She opens one and peruses it as she speaks.)

MINA

I have just a few hurried lines from Jonathan in Transylvania. But his words seem somehow removed and distant. Not like him at all. He says he is well. Or at least he was when he wrote a fortnight ago. He should be returning in a week or so.

LUCY

A fortnight gone? And no clandestine displays of indiscretion? You can tell me, Mina… Have you been kissing your pillow?

MINA

Ah! Lucy! That is private!

(Both giggle.)

MRS. WESTENRA

Privileged information, daughter mine.

MINA

Thank you, Mrs. Westenra. *(To Lucy.)* You must've failed to attend the basic classes in charm school.

MRS. WESTENRA

Well, have *you*, Miss Mina?

MINA

I beg your pardon. Failed to attend charm school?

MRS. WESTENRA

No, silly girl, have you been kissing your pillow?

(Mrs. Westenra and Lucy laugh.)

MINA

Mrs. Westenra! I thought we agreed that is privileged information.

MRS. WESTENRA

Of course, my dear. But, I'm certain you'll
agree. I'm as privileged as they come.

MINA

What about you, Lucy? I hear you've been receiving letters from all sorts of gentlemen. I suppose responding to them has left you no time to answer mine.

LUCY

I must say, you tax me very unfairly with
being a bad correspondent.

MRS. WESTENRA

Indeed, it is unfair Mina. When Lucille was away at boarding school, she always made it a practice to write letters to me. Hundreds of them, she tells me. Pity she never took them down to the postman's box.

LUCY

Most times I had nothing suitable to wear on the walk to the post. A young lady must always look her best. And the weather wouldn't cooperate. Too much sun, it would tarnish my fair skin. Too cloudy, then I can't be seen at all. And what's the point of that?

MINA

Some girls are so vain.

(Lucy and Mina laugh.)

MRS. WESTENRA

Well, men like the women they share a bed with to be fair. They prefer their wives to be naive.

LUCY

Mother, please. Practice what you preach.
Your irreverence is scandalous.

MRS. WESTENRA

Not a whit. In fact, I was always faithful
to my husband. Both of them.

MINA

Mrs. Westenra, you know that Jonathan and I are engaged to be
married. I would love some of your matronly counsel.

MRS. WESTENRA

Well, Dear girl, my advice has always been… Find a man with whom
you can share your thoughts. A man with whom you can be intimate.
And a man with whom his money will be shared. And when you find
him, whatever you do,… Don't tell your husband.

(All laugh.)

LUCY

Mina, don't listen to a word. Mother, you're incorrigible.

MINA

Don't chide your mother, Lucy. I find her point of view refreshing. I
think more ladies should voice their thoughts and feelings about men
openly. We're closing in on the turn of the century, after all. Mark
my words. Women will find themselves their husband's equal
and wind up in the House of Commons!

MRS. WESTENRA

On the contrary, Miss Mina. A wife's place is in the kitchen. It's the best location for poisoning his cup of tea.

MINA

Mrs. Westenra! You didn't!

MRS. WESTENRA

No, of course I didn't, Dear!... Hemlock was out of season.

LUCY

Mother!

MRS. WESTENRA

And Arsenic was too expensive.

MINA

Oh! Thank God, you didn't!

MRS. WESTENRA

At least that's the story I gave to Scotland Yard.

(She stands up too quickly. Becomes momentarily dizzy. The girls rush to her aid.)

LUCY

Mother, careful!

*(The girls rush to her aid. Swales re-enters
having heard Lucy's exclamation.)*

Remember the doctor says you need to stand more slowly. And do
nothing to over-excite yourself.

MRS. WESTENRA

Over excite myself? Please dear. I'm all right, now, girls. I'm fine.

LUCY

Mr. Swales, would you be so kind as to escort Mother to her
bedchamber to rest? Mina and I should like to be alone for a moment.
I've something I'd like to ask of her.

MRS. WESTENRA

Very well, I know when I'm not wanted. But always know this,… You
are a beautiful young lady with qualities befitting the royals. A girl
who can have any man in the world. You are educated, lovely, prim
and proper; the epitome of the modern-day Victorian woman. It has
been my pleasure to stand as your example. When you are married,
I shall shed tears of joy for him, tears of loss for myself. My love for
you, dear child, will remain forever constant.

(Swales grabs the valises.)

LUCY

Why, thank you, Mother. That was beautiful.

(Mrs. Westenra turns back.)

MRS. WESTENRA

I was talking to Mina.

(She exits. Both girls laugh.)

LUCY

That's my Mum.

MINA

I love her so! She's absolutely splendid!

LUCY

Isn't she though.

MINA

I can see where you've refined your rapier wit. Is she all right? Does she have those spells often?

LUCY

Sadly, yes. And lately increasing in severity. Her physician says she has an anomaly of the heart.

MINA

Oh, Dear.

LUCY

She must be careful, is all. No over-exertion.
Avoid all possible shock to the system.

MINA

I pray for her recovery.

LUCY

As do I.

MINA

Now, what is it you wanted to ask me?

LUCY

I have three suitors at once! All vying for my affections. A physician, an aristocrat, and a rancher. If you were me, who would you choose?

MINA

Difficult for me to speak on this, Lucy. I've only one,…. Jonathan Harker. And unfortunately, though I'm awfully happy for you, I'm rather preoccupied with his well-being at present. You can see from his letters how strange he sounds.

LUCY

My! Are those little niceties, scribbled at his signature?

MINA

No, it's not what you think, he's just…

LUCY

Little hearts? Exes? And Ohs? My word, Mina.
What have you two been writing about?

MINA

I told you, nothing. He probably just smeared droplets of ink.

LUCY

Oh, I'm sure!

(Lucy reaches for the letters.)

MINA

Keep away now, Luce!

LUCY

Let's see them.

*(Lucy grabs the letters from Mina's hand
and runs. Mina chases her.)*

MINA

No, Lucy!

LUCY

Why, just look what he's written! You naughty little thing!

(Mina attempts to snatch them back.)

MINA

Lucy! Give them back! They're private!

(They begin circling the stage as a game of "cat and mouse".)

LUCY

After I've read them all.

MINA

Come back here, you ninny!

(Lucy begins her exit from the scene.)

LUCY

Catch me first!

MINA

Oh, I will, you Strumpet!

(Mina cuts her off and is able to grab the love letter away from Lucy. She then tucks it into her bodice.)

LUCY

Ah! Mina, that's not very nice. Won't you
read a little something to me?

MINA

Very well. I can share this one with you.

(She pulls out a different letter.)

This is the first I received upon his arrival at the Count's home. He describes his steps to the great doors, then the letter ends somewhat abruptly. *(She opens and begins reading. Harker and Coachman enter on opposite side.)* "In the gloom the castle looked of considerable size, and as several dark ways led from it under great, round arches it perhaps seemed bigger than it really is. As I approached two great doors, old and studded with large iron nails, and set in a projecting portcullis of massive stone. I stood in silence where I was, for I did not know what to do. What sort of place had I come to? I heard a heavy step approaching behind the great doors; and saw through the...

(Mina's voice trails off as the two exit. Harker picks up...)

[END OF SCENE]

Scene 3

"The Castle Dracula"

[Carpathians, Transylvania]

(As darker music leads in, lights gradually rise on the castle wherein ambient glow warms the areas of the outer doors and the upper door at the top of the grand staircase. The set is designed in such a way that the audience can view the two large medieval exterior doors and the interior of the domicile simultaneously. A haze of fog comes rolling in as we see a carriage approach and then come to a complete halt. Harker steps off of the carriage as he continues writing his letter with quill and parchment. The Coachman carries both Harker's suitcase and his valise, one in each hand. Throughout suspenseful music,...

<u>HARKER</u>

(The moment just before Mina and Lucy exit and are out of sight, Mina continues to move her lips but without sound as Harker writes on a piece of parchment. He speaks aloud, picking up where Mina left off in a "shared line". We are to believe he is speaking the very words he is writing in his letter to Mina. The transition should be smooth and flawless and the audience should intuit that we've now bumped back in time about a month in order to experience Jonathan's arrival at the castle.)

…chinks the gleam of a coming light. Then there was the sound of rattling chains and the clanking of massive bolts drawn back. A key was turned with the loud grating noise of a long disuse, and the great doors swung back. Till I write again. Yours. Jonathan."

(Harker quickly folds the letter, stuffs it into a previously addressed envelope to Mina at her home near London. Then he hands the post to the Coachman, presumably for the driver to deliver the letter at the appropriate postal point. The Coachman, with great nervousness snatches the letter as the Count comes into view. He hops back onto the carriage and drives away briskly into the night.

Harker tentatively steps up to the doors. He looks about him from time to time. He pulls his coat collar upward as he gets a sudden chill. He reaches to one of the over-sized door knockers on the portal and gives three solid raps to alert the inhabitant to his arrival. He waits. The interior, gothic-arched door at the uppermost level opens ever so slowly. An almost supernatural light bleeds from within. An old man in full black enters, holding a lit candelabra. Once he leaves the door, he waves his bony hand and magically the wooden door closes behind him. He descends what appears to be an endless series of stone steps until he arrives at the large castle doors. They open slowly, pulling inward, and the Count is seen standing center, not having actually touched either door with his hands.)

DRACULA
Good evening.

HARKER
Good evening, Sir. I am Jonathan Harker, Solicitor from England. My apologies if I have arrived sooner than expected. My driver flew like a ghost in the night.

DRACULA

'Denn die todten reiten schnell'. For the dead travel fast.

HARKER

Yes, so I've heard.

DRACULA

Welcome to my home. Enter freely and of your own will. Careful where you step. It is an old castle. Its floors and thresholds are… enigmatic. Come freely, go safely, and leave something of the happiness you bring.

HARKER

Thank you, Count. You are a most gracious host.

DRACULA

I am Dracula and I bid you welcome, Mr. Harker, to this castle. You may come and go as you wish.

(Dracula waves a hand at the double doors behind his guest. The two grand medieval locks turn by his dark wizardry and bolt into place with an echoing thunder. Harker, oblivious to what just happened, hears the sound and turns to see the doors now closed. He is nonplussed.)

HARKER

It is certainly a secure dwelling.

DRACULA

Make yourself to home. The night air is chill and you must eat, rest, and warm yourself by the fire.

(Dracula sets the candelabra upon the dining table.)

HARKER

Surely, you don't mean to wait upon me hand
and foot yourself. Have you no servants?

(As Jonathan removes his scarf, overcoat, and hat, the Count receives them and hangs each personal effect respectfully on a coat rack throughout the following dialogue.)

DRACULA

Sir, you are my guest. It is late and my people are not… available. Let me see to your comforts myself.

HARKER

Thank you, Good Count.

DRACULA

You will need, after your journey, to refresh yourself by cloth and basin upstairs. I trust you will find all you wish. For now, I pray you, be seated and sup how you please. You will find your repast prepared. Behold…

*(The Count removes the silver lid of a hot dish.
Beneath is a beautifully prepared meal.)*

DRACULA

Excellent roast Chicken Paprika, aged cheese, a blend of fresh vegetables, Mamaliga, and a sweet wine. A vintage bottle of Tokay.

HARKER

Only one chalice, Count? Will you not join me?

DRACULA

I never drink... wine.

(Dracula opens an ornate little chest on the table. It contains a knife, fork, and spoon resting upon a velveteen cushion. He places each at Harker's place setting. Harker gracefully tucks a cloth napkin into his collar, takes knife and fork in hand, and begins to eat.)

HARKER

Your hospitality is most humbling. Will you not dine as well?

DRACULA

You will, I trust, excuse me that I do not join you, but I have dined already and I do not sup.

(Sound of wolves howling stridently just outside the castle walls.)

HARKER

Oh, good Lord, what is that?!

DRACULA

Yes, listen to them. Children of the night. What music they make!

HARKER

Pardon me, good host, if I share not the same enthusiasm?

*(Dracula is slightly amused that Harker is
uneasy and cracks a subtle smile.)*

DRACULA

Do the wolves frighten you?

HARKER

Well, it's only, we don't get many a wolf upon
the cobblestones of Baker Street.

DRACULA

A pity. Ah, sir, you dwellers in the city cannot enter into the feelings of the hunter. Come, tell me of the house, which you have procured for me.

*(Harker wipes his mouth, reaches into his
valise and withdraws a document.)*

HARKER

Ah, yes. The estate is in Whitby. It is surrounded by a high wall, of ancient structure, built of heavy stones. Somewhat dilapidated, it has not been repaired for a number of years. It is in places, gloomy. There is a deep, dark-looking pond. The house is very large, dating back to the medieval period. It is heavily barred with iron.

DRACULA

It sounds perfect for my,… purposes.

HARKER

It is a rather ancient place.

DRACULA

That is better for me. I am glad that it is old and large. I myself am of an old family. And to live in a new house would… kill me. We Transylvanian nobles love not to think that our bones may lie among the common dead. The darkness of the house appeals to me. For, look about you. The walls of my castle are broken, the shadows are many, and the wind breathes cold through the crumbling battlements and casings. I love the shade and the shadows.

(Harker continues eating.)

HARKER

Well, you will feel at home then, in your new dwelling.

DRACULA

I am certain of it.

HARKER

I am bound by my profession to disclose to you
that there is also an institution nearby.

DRACULA

Institution?

HARKER

Whitby Asylum. A secure imprisonment for maniacal deviants,
depraved lunatics, and the criminally insane.

DRACULA

They sound like nice enough neighbors.

HARKER

Well I wouldn't recommend planning a garden party…

(Harker accidentally cuts a finger.)

HARKER

Oh, my word! I seem to have nicked my forefinger. Forgive my
clumsiness, please. I'm bleeding a bit.

*(Dracula is drawn to Harker's wound. He
clearly shows the pangs of temptation.)*

DRACULA

Take care. Take care how you cut yourself. It is more dangerous than you think in this country.

(The Count hands Harker a cloth handkerchief.)

HARKER

Thank you, I will.

DRACULA

You must be tired. Your bedchamber is ready and tomorrow you will sleep as late as you wish. I shall be... *away* till the afternoon.

HARKER

You certainly have a home of beautiful artifacts. Have you no concern of robbers? Thieves who may,... uh,...

DRACULA

Steal from me? Take my possessions?

HARKER

Well, I only meant,...

DRACULA

I know what you meant. A very long time ago, I had my belongings, my family, my life, everything that I cherish taken from me.

HARKER

I'm sorry. I didn't know. I trust those thieves have
been rightly confined and prosecuted.

(An eerie music eases in to underscore Dracula's following passages. All about him lights fade and a red glowing light comes up gradually, illuminating the Count who grows increasingly angry, defensive, defiant.)

DRACULA

What do you know about it? How does one begin to express a lifetime's existence of persecution? My family, my people, the Szekelys, were a proud race. We bore down from Iceland, the fighting spirit of Thor. But the Turks poured their thousands upon our frontiers. We were beaten down upon a bloody field. Their warlike fury swept the earth like a living flame. We thought the werewolves themselves had come. Like ancient witches who had mated with devils in the desert, they sought to destroy us. But what devil or witch was ever so great as Attila, whose blood flows through these veins?! I would not rest until I'd tasted their blood upon our swords!

HARKER

Your people were brave.

DRACULA

Brave?! I demanded it! My fellow countrymen, Romanians of old, the common peasants were divided. And I, a Dracul, had to unify Transylvania to protect it. So, I threatened every man, woman, and child with torture beyond imagination if they would not join me. If they did not rise and fight to the death, under my rule, they would suffer a fate worse than Hell itself! Yes, there were dissenters. And mere intimidation would no longer suffice. So, I had to *teach* them to obey.

HARKER
How?

DRACULA

We invaded their camps in the dark of night, blinded them, nailed them one to another. Their precious children were pulled apart by horses. We left them writhing in agony amongst the flames of scorched earth. You understand, I did this for my people. I had no choice. We could only rise to ultimate power if Romania swore undying allegiance to me.

It did. So this was the Dracula who saw an entire nation of Turks impaled upon a forest of crimson. And I myself drove the spikes!

HARKER
I believe I'm finished with dinner.

DRACULA

You must think me an eccentric old man. But, you see, Mr. Harker, to a Szekely, a Dracul, the pride of his house and name springs eternal. And therefore I say "Woe be unto him that will come into my home, feast of my table, rest his skull upon my pillows, and wrong me!" To steal my possessions, to desecrate my name, is to incur the wrath of a thousand years. I would, while he were sleeping like a babe, drag him by the throat to an alter! As a lamb to be slaughtered. And I would prove his butcher!...

(Lighting restores and music ends. There is silence.)

__DRACULA__

Sleep well, my friend. And pleasant dreams.

(Music. Dracula takes Harker's eating utensils, places them back into the small ornate chest. [The purpose for this is so that Harker will not have access to a knife or other implements which may be used against the old count.] Dracula exits. As Dracula ascends the staircase, he waves a hand at the door to his room. It magically opens. Once he passes through, it closes behind him. A beat, and then Harker rises to ascend the steps to his bedchamber. He stops, turns to look at the castle doors. He goes to them in haste and attempts to turn the handles. They are locked in place. He attempts to shoulder the doors open to no avail. He realizes he is trapped. Defeated, he grabs his bags and heads to his bedchamber. He exits into a gothic arched doorway in his room, presumably, the privy. Music leads us into the next scene.)

[END OF SCENE]

Scene 4

"Madness, Examined"

[Whitby Asylum]

(Whitby Asylum. Enter Dr. Seward with a large hypodermic needle, followed by Waites Simmons, Renfield's attendant, with a chain, Smollet Snelling, a young nurse with a tray of food, and Patti Hennessey, an older nurse.)

<u>SEWARD</u>

…The case of Renfield grows more interesting as I get to understand the man. He has certain qualities very largely developed. He seems to have some settled scheme of his own. But what it is, I do not yet know.

<u>SNELLING</u>

In layman's terms, Doctor Seward?

<u>SIMMONS</u>

He's off his nut.

<u>SEWARD</u>

This morning we had to transfer him to solitary. This is why I need to assign the three of you to his care. At present, he must be restrained in order that I can administer an injection of opiate. He needs to sleep.

HENNESSEY

Dr. Seward, if I may ask,... Why was he transferred to solitary?

SEWARD

Mr. Renfield has become delusional. He has some idea that by ingesting insects he can protect and prolong his life. This morning Simmons and I caught him with a mouthful.

SNELLING

Full of... what, exactly?

SIMMONS

Clenched his teeth, he did. We pried open his jaw with an iron crow. His maw was over-run, crawlin' with ants, gnats, fleas, and termites. He said it would keep him from dyin'.

SEWARD

Occasionally, he refers to himself in the third person and threatens to increase his consumption of vermin to cockroaches and mice.

SIMMONS

He can have 'em.

SEWARD

Simmons, you will take possession of the key to his cell. Miss Snelling, you will bring the man his meals. Thrice daily. Mrs. Hennessey, you will be responsible for his baths. For now, the hypodermic is ready. Miss Snelling, stand further off beyond the length of his tether. Simmons, grab hold of the chain and mind his strength.

SIMMONS

Yes, Doctor.

SNELLING

Is he dangerous, Dr. Seward?

(Low, foreboding music eases in.)

SEWARD

They *all* are, Smollet… All of them… Mr. Simmons?

(Simmons unlocks the door to the cell.)

SIMMONS

All right, then, Mr. Renfield! Wakey-
wakey! The doctor is in to see you!

(As music increases in volume, we see a dark figure, large and hulking, slowly stirring from within the cell. It is in black silhouette as there is a ghastly green light glowing from within. Once Renfield emerges, we see how disheveled, filthy, and large he is. He appears to tower over the three hospital employees. There is a palpable sense of tension and danger in the air. The musically-orchestrated build-up to Renfield's entrance is almost humorous. It stops suddenly.)

RENFIELD

Someone called?... Dr. Seward and friends! Welcome to Renfield's humble abode. Now that these are my new 'accommodations', you don't come around much anymore. You avoid your patients as one would the very mouth of Hell. Which brings to mind a simple riddle. When might one *not* avoid the very mouth of Hell? *Omnia romae vernalia sunt* – Hell has its price.

SEWARD

Very good, Mr. Renfield. I've come to administer
an injection. It will help you to sleep.

RENFIELD

Dr. Seward, Governor of Whitby Asylum. Why have you brought your attendants here? To witness your expertise with a stark-raving lunatic? A madman? Renfield knows what you say about him; Great physical strength; morbidly excitable; periods of gloom; possibly dangerous, probably malicious, and zoophagous!

SEWARD

Mr. Renfield, your collection of flies must go. It is unsanitary. Simmons, fetch a rubbish bin.

REFIELD

Oh, no! Dr. Seward, they are just now fattening up nicely on clumps of sugar! Then, they'll be ready to feed to my spiders. Might Renfield have three days? He will clear them away!

SEWARD

We will discuss this at length after you've had proper rest.

SNELLING

I've brought you some food, Mr. Renfield.

RENFIELD

Thank you, no, Miss. Mr. Renfield has already dined. But I'm sure Dr. Seward has revealed to you, my 'special' diet. Dear Doctor, that reminds me… Might I have a kitten, a nice, little, sleek, playful kitten? That I can play with and teach and feed, and feed, and feed?

SEWARD

Would you not rather a cat than a kitten?

RENFIELD

Oh, yes! I would like a cat! I only asked for a
kitten lest you should refuse me the larger.

SEWARD

I shall refuse you both, lest you forget who is in power here.

RENFIELD

Oh, but you are sorely mistaken. Thou art but a worm, mere mortal. There is a power greater than all powers and he will arrive in time.

SEWARD

What do you mean, Renfield? Who will arrive?

RENFIELD

The Master! The Master is coming!

SIMMONS

Shall I secure his restraints now, Doctor?

SEWARD

Please.

RENFIELD

Too bad about the girl. She'll choose
another. And you'll be left to pine.

SEWARD

How do you know of her? Who told you?

RENFIELD

It's all right. We've all nasty habits, personal demons. Yours is the
pining after a love you'll never have. Mine is the ingestation of insect
larvae, the taste of fetid slugs crawling within carrion carcasses,
the slip-slurping of live maggots into the vortex of my throat… But
you, yours is a sickness of the heart. You see, I know all sorts of
things now!

SEWARD

Trouble yourself not, Mr. Renfield. It is time for your injection. You
need to sleep this evening.

(Suddenly, just as Seward has approached Renfield with the needle, the lunatic bursts into a spontaneous rage of madness. He is able to toss the needle away and wrap part of his restraint chains around Seward's neck. Simmons and Snelling panic.)

RENFIELD

NO!!! NO!!! SLEEP THAT KNITS UP THE RAVELL'D SLEEVE OF CARE!, TO SLEEP, PERCHANCE TO DREAM!!!!

(Simmons attempts to help loosen the chain from around Seward's neck, but to no avail.)

SEWARD

For God's sake, Simmons! You can't fight his strength! Go get the syringe! Prick him and push the plunger until the fluid is gone!

RENFIELD

GLAMIS HATH MURDERED SLEEP! RENFIED SHALL SLEEP NO MORE! RENFIELD SHALL SLEEP NO MORE!!!

(Simmons does as he is instructed, he grabs the syringes, jabs the patient and plunges the fluid.)

RENFIELD

Cast your troubles away to sleep,
And drive the needle in two inches deep!
Push, push, that fluid to the brim,
Till you've lost your flesh to a death's head grin.

(Renfield releases his hold upon Seward.
He becomes docile quite quickly.)

<u>RENFIELD</u>

Nighty-night, Dr. Seward. May God or… *whomever*, have mercy upon your soul! My salvation is assured.

(Music. Simmons, Snelling, Hennessey, and Seward manipulate the chains that pull Renfield back into the small cell. Snelling leaves the tray of food with him, just in case. He is locked back inside. Exit the doctor and his attendants. Music plays out into the following scene.)

[END OF SCENE]

Scene 5

"Twas a Rough Night"

[Carpathians, Transylvania]

(The Castle Dracula. Music eases in, intensely evil in quality. Harker is seen restlessly stirring in his bed. Enter, amidst red light and billowing fog, three women in white. They are beautiful and at the same time un-nerving. It is clear that they are of the undead as the pallor of their skin glows a milky hue of near-blue. They have fangs, razor-sharp. Their flowing, white gowns are suggestively sensual. They reach the bed chamber of Jonathan Harker and fix their eyes upon him. He appears to see them, but becomes paralyzed and mute. He is clearly frightened to death.)

WOMAN-IN-WHITE #1
Go on! You are first, and we shall follow.

WOMAN-IN-WHITE #2
The right is yours to begin.

WOMAN-IN-WHITE #3
He is young and strong.

WOMAN-IN-WHITE #1
There are kisses for us all.

WOMAN-IN-WHITE #2

Let us take him together.

WOMAN-IN-WHITE #3

Come, Sisters!

(They surround Harker. He fights to break free of his invisible bonds, but cannot. Each woman goes to a different area of his body as though to begin biting and feeding upon his flesh, One goes to an arm, the other to a foot, and the third to his neck. The moment that they all place their mouths upon him, a blast of fire issues from within the chamber and Dracula appears. He is enraged. The women are startled. They hold from feasting. Yet they stay connected to Harker. They cower beneath the power of their Lord.)

DRACULA

How dare you touch him! Any of you! How dare you cast eyes on him, when I had forbidden it! Back! I tell you all! This one belongs to me! Beware how you meddle with him or you'll suffer a reckoning with your dark Lord!

(The three of them laugh in evil tones.)

WOMAN-IN-WHITE #1

You yourself never loved.

WOMAN-IN-WHITE #2

You do not love!

WOMAN-IN-WHITE #3

You cannot love!

(The three laugh louder.)

DRACULA

Yes, I too, can love. You yourselves can tell it from the past. Is it not so? Well, now I promise you that when I am done with him, you may have him as you please. Now go! GO! I must awaken him, for there is much work to be done.

WOMAN-IN-WHITE #1

And us?

WOMAN-IN-WHITE #2

What are we to do?

WOMAN-IN-WHITE #3

Are we to have nothing tonight?

WOMAN-IN-WHITE #1

Not so much as a morsel of flesh?

(Music. Dracula produces a cloth sack and tosses it at the women's feet. The cry of an infant is heard. They open the bag, look within, and smile with delight. They take it with them as they vanish through a window. The echoing of the crying child and the laughter of the women fills the castle halls, as Dracula waves a hand over Harker's body and gradually withdraws from the

bedchamber. As music continues, Harker, as if in a state of sleep, finds his way to the library. Whereupon, there is a small table and a pile of books. He collapses upon them. A beat. Lights rise and music subtly changes to indicate morning. Harker is seen hunched over on the table, his aching head buried within the pile of books. Enter Dracula dressed differently than the previous evening. He seemingly appears from nowhere. He startles Harker who does not hear him approach.)

DRACULA

Good morning, Mr. Harker.

HARKER

Oh! Good Heavens, but you gave me a
start! I didn't hear you come in.

DRACULA

My apologies. I did not mean to startle you.

HARKER

That's,… all right.

DRACULA

I trust you had a good night's rest.

HARKER

No, in fact I did not.

DRACULA

So sorry to hear. What troubled you so?

HARKER

I was kept awake by… nightmares.

DRACULA

Nightmares? More than one?

HARKER

Yes. Three, to be exact.

DRACULA

The stuff of a troubled mind. Well, I am glad you found your way in here. I am sure here is much that will interest you. *(Referring to his books).* These *friends* have been good to me and for some years past, ever since I had the idea of traveling to London, have given me many, many hours of pleasure.

HARKER

Count, if I may ask. You never said *why* you wished to move to London. It seems a strangely curious plan to make for a man in your position here in Transylvania. Why this relocation?

DRACULA

It is a fair question. You see, I am in business with a Doctor of Botany. He is experimenting with the growth of English flora beneath foreign soil. I wanted to see the world one last time before

I am too old. So, I agreed to facilitate the shipment of seven crates of Transylvanian soil to be dispersed. These seven boxes will be delivered to Whitby, Carfax, and Exeter, where the botanist will commence his work.

HARKER

What an odd experiment.

DRACULA

The man is a scientist. This botanical expert seeks to discover how English-grown foliage might survive and react to soil from Romania. His plant subjects are largely indigenous to England such as; Meadowsweet, Flowering Heather, and Rosa Arvensis. I shall 'over-see' the shipping myself. And once I arrive, I may stay for an indefinite period of time,… if all goes well.

HARKER

If all goes well?

DRACULA

Yes, depending upon whether or not the crated earth from Transylvania can,… 'preserve' that which is buried deep within England's ground.

HARKER

I understand.

DRACULA

Please, feel free to help yourself to my library.

HARKER

I don't feel very much like reading at present.

DRACULA

Tomorrow my friend, we must part.

HARKER

We? Are we to travel together?

DRACULA

No, Mr. Harker. You will return to England straightaway. I must stay behind to supervise the loading of the seven crates of soil.

HARKER

And my letters home?

DRACULA

They have been dispatched.

HARKER

I have a few more.

DRACULA

Of course. Would you have them sent by standard service? Or express?

(Harker pulls a stack of envelopes out of an inner pocket and hands them to Dracula. Harker momentarily turns his back to the Count.)

HARKER

Post-haste, please. Expediency is critical.

(The Count steps deliberately to a lit candelabra. He takes Harker's letters, places them in the flame and they go up all at once in a small ball of fire. This effect is to be done with 'flash paper'. The timing is such that Harker turns back to the Count the moment the letters have been extinguished. The entire movement should be done matter-of-factly. Dracula should never show his 'cards' as someone nervous about doing this action in secret. Harker should never detect anything unusual has happened. For the effect to work best, it must be choreographed to be played swiftly and smoothly. Dracula may place a hand inside an inner pocket as if to pretend to stash Harker's letters there.)

DRACULA

They'll be sent off in a flash.

HARKER

Thank you, Count.

DRACULA

Now, tomorrow I will not be here. But all will be ready for your journey. In the morning come the Szgany and Slovaks to load the crates onto wagons for a cargo ship. When they have gone, my carriage will come for you. Then bear you to the Borgo

Pass to meet the diligence from Bukovina to Bistriz. But I am in hopes that I will see more of you at my new Castle Dracula in Whitby.

(Dracula turns to leave.)

HARKER

Why may I not leave now?

(Dracula stops in his tracks. He turns back to face Harker.)

DRACULA

Because, dear sir, it is not yet light and my
coachman and horses are away on a mission.

HARKER

But I would walk with pleasure.

DRACULA

Why is that?

HARKER

I want to get away at once.

DRACULA

And your baggage?

HARKER

I do not care about it.

DRACULA

But your personal effects.

HARKER

I can send for them some other time.

DRACULA

Very well. You English have a saying which is close to my heart. For its spirit is that which rules our Boyars; *"Welcome the coming, and speed the parting guest".* Come with me, my dear young friend. Not a minute more shall you wait in my house against your will. Though, sad I am at your going. And that you so suddenly desire it. Come!

(A flash of lightning.)

HARKER

Where are we going?

DRACULA

To the entrance door, of course.

(Dracula opens the door. Crashing thunder followed by the howling of wolves can be heard.)

HARKER

Oh, my.

DRACULA

Hark! The howling of many wolves. They are hungry and must be fed. Well, on your way, Mr. Harker.

HARKER

The wolves, they sound close at hand.

DRACULA

If you are fast, you've nothing to fear.

HARKER

Close the door! I will wait until afternoon!

DRACULA

But you were so insistent on leaving.

HARKER

I was, yes.

DRACULA

Very well. You are right. It is best you stay. It is not,... safe in the "forest beyond". I will lock us up securely within the castle once again. *(He closes the door and begins throwing the locks back into place.)* We want nothing to get in,...

*(He inconspicuously leers at Harker for a
moment. Harker is oblivious to this.)*

…and nothing to get out.

*(Harker does not hear his comment. Dracula
returns his attention to the door.)*

I will leave you to your liberties. It is near
light. I must retire to my chamber.

*(Lighting and thunder. Dracula exits. Music. Once Harker knows
that the strange old man is out of sight, he goes about looking for a
way to escape. He takes a spear from the wall, attempts to pry the
door open but to no avail. The women in white appear in smoke and
catch him attempting to escape. They pursue him as he does his
beast to stave them off. He then runs up the staircase to an area at
the upper-most floor. He sees a small gothic-arched stained glass
window. He is able to pry it open. He squeezes out, steps outside
upon a ledge, just as the women reach him. Just as his foot is nearly
out of the window, it is grabbed by one of the vampires. But he slips
through. The three women stay at the window, reaching for him,
hissing, salivating. Harker leaps across to a nearby turret of the
castle. He uses stones, cracks, and crevices in the cylindrical column
as hand and foot holds and is able to climb his way down. As the
wolves' howling increases in volume, Harker flees into the wood. He
has escaped the Castle Dracula.)*

[END OF SCENE]

Scene 6

"Dance Card"

[Whitby, England]

(Warm, sunny lighting and pleasant music convey the following day in an altogether different place. We have returned to the garden cemetery. Enter Lucy and Mina. They are chasing each other and laughing their way into the scene. The garden is suddenly alive with youth and joy. Lucy goes to pick a flower or two. Mina, with journal and quill, sits upon the stone bench. She writes a letter. Enter Mrs. Westenra with a calling card in her hand. Dr. John Seward follows her, closely behind.)

MRS. WESTENRA

Lucy, Dear? *(Reading the card.)* A Doctor John Seward to see you.

LUCY

Thank you, Mother. Welcome him here.

(Mrs. Westenra gestures that Seward may follow her into the garden, then she hands the calling card to Lucy. Mrs. Westenra exits. Lucy speaks to Seward.)

LUCY

Won't you come to the garden?

SEWARD

Good afternoon, Miss Lucy. Do you remember me?

LUCY

Why, of course! You're the "lunatic-asylum-man"!

SEWARD

Yes, I suppose that's one way to put it.

LUCY

So, my mother said you wanted to see me. Please, no beating around the bush. Spill out your thoughts as a river doth its crystalline waters. But, if you please, do so on a topic of my choosing. Which is,... Define 'love'.

(Nervously, Dr. Seward fidgets with a lancet during the following.)

SEWARD

Well,... very well, Miss Lucy. Science dictates that in order to populate the firmament, beings of opposite sex must couple as a means to propagate... First, however, there are the social mores of modern-day London. These are typified by the laws of attraction, a period of courtship, followed by a matrimonial commencement. Only then, can the two species engage in consummation, a nature-driven response resulting in reproduction.

LUCY

Why that's beautiful, Dr. Seward. So,...
elegant. And so very... clinical.

MRS. WESTENRA

Oh, Lucy Dear!

LUCY

Yes, Mother?!

MRS. WESTENRA

Sir Arthur Holmwood. Son of the Lord
and Lady Godalming to see you.

LUCY

Thank you, Mother. Welcome him here.
If you'll excuse me, Doctor.

*(Lucy goes to a piazza to meet with Holmwood. Mrs. Westenra
gestures that Holmwood may follow her to the piazza, then she
hands the calling card to Lucy. Mrs. Westenra exits. Lucy speaks to
Holmwood.)*

LUCY

Why you're looking dapper today, Arthur.

HOLMWOOD

Miss Lucy, you are beautiful as always.

LUCY

Won't you join me on the piazza?

HOLMWOOD

My pleasure.

LUCY

I understand your father, the Lord Godalming,
has taken ill. I trust it's not serious.

HOLMWOOD

Unfortunately, it appears critical.

LUCY

Oh dear. I'm so sorry, Arthur.

HOLMWOOD

Thank you for your concern, Lucille. Father spends more time in bed
than out. But Mother is with him. She waits on him hand and foot.
It doesn't look good.

LUCY

I will include him in my nightly prayers. Now, I have a question.
Would you be so kind as to respond?

HOLMWOOD

I will do my best.

LUCY

What would you say, is a proper definition of 'Love'?

HOLMWOOD

Oh dear. Definition of … 'Love', is it? Well, I suppose… When two people,… a man and a woman… They,… actually enjoy time together? And then ultimately they may steal away to a private location,… Where they may actually, in private,…

(He looks about him to insure no one is within ear shot.)

…hold hands.

LUCY

Oh my. Isn't that a naughty notion.

MRS. WESTENRA

Oh, Lucy Dear!

LUCY

I'll return.

(As she leaves Holmwood at the piazza...)

LUCY

Yes, Mother?

MRS. WESTENRA

A Mr. Quincy Morris to see you.

LUCY

Welcome him here.

MRS. WESTENRA

(A forced smile.)

They're beginning to pile up, Love.

(Lucy follows her mother to yet another area of the garden to meet with Mr. Morris. Mrs. Westenra is seen gesturing an introduction of Morris to Lucy. She then turns to have a seat alone at another area of the garden where she sits, opens a parasol, and daubs her forehead with a lacy hanky. Lucy and Quincy stay at the stone bench. Quincy, as a gentleman would, gestures for Lucy to sit on the bench while he hikes a booted foot on the bench and lights a cigar.)

MORRIS

Miss Lucy, I know I ain't good enough to regulate the fixins of your little shoes, but I guess if you wait till you find one who is, he'd be one lucky son of a buck and start ta grinnin' like a mule eatin' briars.

LUCY

Thank you, Mr. Morris. That was probably a very lovely thing to say… Oh, gentlemen? If you will,… What can I do for you all?

ALL

MISS LUCY, WILL YOU MARRY ME?

(Lucy grabs her mother by the arm and
brings her downstage, sotto voce.)

LUCY

Mother, I feel so sorry for the other two fellows.

MRS. WESTENRA

Which two?

LUCY

I haven't decided yet.

MRS. WESTENRA

Well, you'd better hurry, Dear. They're all three aging as we speak.

LUCY

(Aside.)

What a conundrum. I feel so miserable…
And that makes me so very happy!

(Delightful dance music of appropriate period and place begins. It is light and airy. Lucy begins dancing with Seward, then Morris cuts in as Mina goes to Seward and they dance, then Holmwood cuts in on Lucy and Morris, then begins to dance with Lucy as Morris takes Mrs. Westenra by the hand and dances with her. Three couples now dance together in the cemetery garden. It is a beautifully choreographed trio of period dance, polite, proper, and well-executed. Music comes to an end and so does the dance. All six applaud the fun they

have just had. Lucy takes Holmwood by the hand and brings him center.)

<u>LUCY</u>
Sir Arthur Holmwood, I accept!

They kiss. All others are good sports and applaud, then escort their respective dance partners out of the scene as more serious and ominous music eases in to announce the coming Demeter.)

[END OF SCENE]

Scene 7

"Voyage of the Demeter"

[The Baltic Sea]

(In a blast of exciting music depicting sea voyage, actors enter the center stage area and one by one, as Russian seamen, begin to "assemble" the ship, DEMETER. It is a Russian vessel, a schooner from Varna. This assembly is done at a fast clip and while the props and set pieces are being placed, the scene should read as deckhands preparing for departure. The entire process should be carefully choreographed in such a way that it appears the crewmen are assisting one another in loading the boat with cargo. Essential items are; a mounted ship's steering wheel down front and center, an old wooden barrel or two, several steamer and cam-back trunks, and the seven crates (presumably holding Transylvanian soil), one crate is a coffin. Several long masts with sails attached are hoisted. Dracula bursts from the upright coffin-shaped crate, kills the seamen one by one, and tosses many into the ocean. Scene ends as lights fade and music subsides.)

[END OF SCENE]

Scene 8

"Escape"

[Whitby Asylum]

(Music. Whitby Asylum. Renfield's cell. Present are Renfield, Seward, Simmons, Hennessey, and Snelling. Renfield calls out of his barred window facing the forest.)

RENFIELD

Your new home! Master! Ye have arrived!

SIMMONS

Now, just settle down there, Mr. Renfield.

HENNESSEY

Some strange and sudden change in him, Sir.

SNELLING

About eight of the clock, he began to sniff
around as a dog might when setting.

RENFIELD

(To Seward)

I don't want to talk to you. You don't count
anymore. The master is at hand.

SEWARD

It is some sort of religious mania that has seized him.

RENFIELD

Infinitesimal distinctions between man and man are too paltry an exercise for an omnipotent being. How you madmen give yourselves away! Oh, if you only knew what is in store from the Master of all!

SIMMONS

He's clearly deranged.

RENFIELD

Oh, yes. The lunatic gives himself away, does he not? A shifty look within the eyes when a madman hath seized an idea? A movement of the head and back, which asylum attendant have come to know so well.

HENNESSEY

What have you done with your vermin? Where're they hiding?

RENFIELD

Bother them all. I don't care a pin about them. The wedding maidens rejoice the eyes that await the coming of the bride; yet when the bride draweth nigh, then the maidens shine not to the eyes that are filled.

SEWARD

What is this nonsensical riddle? Explain.

RENFIELD

No vermin here. You may look for yourself.

SNELLING

What? You don't mean to tell us you've given up spiders?!

RENFIELD

Perhaps. But I've not given up petty thievery.

(With this, Renfield tosses a handful of coins onto the stone floor in front of him. In addition are Seward's pocket watch, Simmon's whistle on a chain, Snelling's eating utensils, and Hennessey's pewter container of talcum powder. They all react immediately, down to the floor to recover their personal items, coins included. While they are momentarily distracted, Renfield unlocks his cell with Simmons' key.)

ALL

Oh my! There's my talc! What's all this?
Who's money? How'd he do it?!

(He steps out of the cell.)

RENFIELD

By the way, Mr. Simmons, you may want your jail keys returned!

(Suspense music in. He tosses the keys to the floor and runs off stage, escaping his confines.)

RENFIELD

RENFIELD'S COMING, MASTER!
COMING TO DO YOUR BIDDING!

SEWARD

He's escaped! Hurry, Simmons! Let's after him. Miss Hennessey,
Miss Snelling, alert the asylum staff!

(They split up and run offstage. Exeunt.)

[END OF SCENE]

Scene 9

"Servitude"

[A Forest Between the Asylum and the Cottage]

(A sudden emergence of mysterious music. Dracula appears from the forest, he intercepts Renfield. The music underscores the following dialogue.)

DRACULA

Well, well, well. If it isn't Mr. Renfield. The poorest excuse for a sniveling coward of pseudo-humanity. You are the lowest order of your fellow mortals. You are a mere lunatic and you wreak with the stench of rotted carp.

RENFIELD

Your kind words flow through me. You have
adorned me with a flattery beyond measure.

DRACULA

It is all well-deserved.

RENFIELD

I am here to do your bidding, Master.

DRACULA

You come most carefully upon your hour.

RENFIELD

Aye, but chide Renfield not, please, good
paramour. He is present, nonetheless.

DRACULA

So you are.

RENFIELD

Renfield is your slave.

DRACULA

So too you have become.

RENFIELD

You will reward him. For he has been faithful.

DRACULA

Have you?

RENFIELD

Renfield has worshipped you long and from afar. Now that you are
near, he awaits your commands.

DRACULA

I have only one at present, Renfield.

RENFIELD

Anything, Lord and conqueror.

DRACULA

Go to the bedchamber of one 'Lucy Westenra'. You will know the way. Her French windows are locked. The room has been sanctified and without invitation, I can not enter. But you can. Find your way to her upon the hour of her slumber. Unlock the portal from within. Leave without detection. So that I may have access to her. I will cast open the windows and summon her into the garden cemetery... It is time. Go.

RENFIELD

Renfield will. You will not pass him by. Will you, dear Master, in your distribution of good things?

DRACULA

Do this for me, Slave. And I will bestow
upon you the greatest of all gifts.

RENFIELD

And what might that be?

DRACULA

Cold, eternal death, amongst a legion of depraved souls.

RENFIELD

Enticing as that sounds, Renfield was hoping for, maybe, something more along the lines of immortality among mountains of gold.

DRACULA

Test me not, Mortal. I will bestow upon you
that which you deserve. Now go!

RENFIELD

Aye, Lord of Darkness! Straightaway!

[END OF SCENE]

Scene 10

"The Beast with Two Backs"

[Lucy's Boudoir, Cottage in Whitby]

(Music of mystery and suspense underscores the entire following scene. Renfield creeps his way through underground crawlspaces. Then, a trap door creaks open in the floor of Lucy's bedchamber where she and Mina are fast asleep in the same bed. There is a warm, glowing light emanating from the trap door hole. It is a mysterious and supernatural light. A hand comes out of the trap holding a lit lantern. It is Renfield. He crawls out and goes to the bed. Renfield leers over the two girls for a moment, then goes to the French doors, unlocks the latch, and crawls back down into the trap door hole, closing the lid behind him. Dracula appears in the mist outside the glass window panes. With a wave of his hands, the doors miraculously open by themselves. He holds out his hands towards the sleeping Lucy as if to summon her. She rises hypnotically and slowly glides to the open doors. She exits to join the Count. He takes her by the hand and leads her into the deep woods. Mina awakens when she finds Lucy missing from beside her. She throws on a coat over her night dress.)

<u>MINA</u>
Lucy? Lucy?!

(She goes to the French door windows, sees them open, then closes them and latches them securely shut. She takes Lucy's housecoat in one hand and an oil lamp from beside the bed in the

other. She uses it to see her way out the house. She goes out into the night in search of Lucy. It is cold. The wind kicks up and thunder begins to roll.)

MINA

Lucy! Lucy! I know you mustn't have gotten far without your house coat! Where are you, Dear? Follow my voice, dear-heart! Lucy!

(All of a sudden, Lucy is seen alone appearing in the cemetery garden. Mina is still far enough away that she cannot quite make out that it is her friend. Lucy goes to a gravestone and kneels. Out of the darkness a werewolf appears. It grabs Lucy, hoists her up into his arms as she falls limp. The wolf bites Lucy upon the throat. Mina does not understand exactly what is happening. Only that Lucy's safety is in peril.)

MINA
OH MY GOD!!!, LUCY!!! NO!!!

(The thing waves a hand as if casting a spell on Mina.)

THE BEAST
You will remember nothing.

(Mina brings her hand to her head and slumps a bit as if feeling faint. After the thing bites, he places Lucy back down on top of the grave. The beast vanishes into the wood. Mina shakes the dizziness from her head and runs to Lucy.)

<u>MINA</u>

Lucy, come to the house this instant! We must go home at once!

(Lucy revives. Mina wraps the house coat about Lucy's shoulders and uses a large pin to close it 'round her neck. She leads Lucy back to the cottage and to bed. Mina places the lamp on the nightstand, removes Lucy's housecoat, takes off her own and helps to guide Lucy back to bed where they both cuddle together off to gradual sleep. Music comes to a gentle close.)

[END OF SCENE]

Scene 11

"A Strange Fever"

[Lucy's Boudoir, Cottage in Whitby]

(Lighting and gentle morning music rise back up on Lucy's boudoir to convey a new morning after the storm. Mina is straightening toiletries on a vanity. Mina gently begins to brush Lucy's hair in an effort to gradually wake her. Lucy stirs, music fades out.)

MINA
Well, good morning, Sleepy Head.

LUCY
How long have I slept?

MINA
I thought it time to awaken you. But I wanted to let you get in a few extra winks this morning.

LUCY
Why? What for?

MINA
You were quite the midnight wanderer.

LUCY

What?

MINA

The adventure of the night seems not to have harmed you.

LUCY

How you speak in riddles. What adventure?

MINA

You don't remember, do you?

LUCY

Don't tell me, somnambulating? Again?

MINA

I'm afraid so.

LUCY

Is it warm in here to you?

MINA

Oh! My word!

LUCY

What is it?

MINA

Your throat!

LUCY

What about it?

MINA

On your neck, there are,... Oh, my word! I must've injured you.

LUCY

You?

MINA

I rapped your shawl about you, then fastened it with a large, safety pin. I must've been careless. For you have two small and distinct wounds.

LUCY

Don't be silly, Mina. I hardly feel it at all.

MINA

I hope it doesn't leave a scar.

(Lucy checks her neck wounds in a hand-held mirror.)

LUCY

Doubtful. The two holes are so small. I wouldn't worry.

MINA

Would you like a bandage?

LUCY

No, silly. That's not necessary. In fact, I fancy them a bit. If nothing else, they may allude to a social life that I have not, yet greatly desire.

MINA

Lucy! You're spoken for now, you naughty little minx…

LUCY

It *really* is warm… I'm telling you, I cannot…

(Lucy begins feeling ill.)

MINA

Luce?

LUCY

I'm all right. Just feeling rather faint at the moment.

MINA

Lie back down.
(She does so and Mina feels her forehead.)

LUCY

Oh my! It's almost,… as if…

MINA

Oh! My Lord! Lucy, your forehead! You're
burning up! You're hot as fire!

LUCY

I'm so weak all of a sudden… Mina, I think I'm slipping away.

MINA

Oh God! No, Lucy! Stay with me. I'll ring Dr. Seward!

(Mina grabs a bell from Lucy's bedside table.)

MINA

He'll hear the bell from across the lawn at
the asylum. Hold tight, my love!

*(Mina goes to the French doors, slings them
open and furiously rings the bell.)*

MINA

He's always up early. He must've heard.

LUCY

Water, please.

MINA

Yes, yes, of course! Here, my love.

(Mina gives Lucy a glass of water.)

LUCY

Bless you, dearest…

(Young Mr. Nigel Billington, a footman of the Westenra cottage, begins knocking on the outside door to Lucy's boudoir.)

(Knocking)

LUCY

Dreams. I'm dreaming again. The Sandman came. He loves me so. Do let him in, won't you, Wilhemina?

MINA

Oh, my poor friend. You've succumbed to delirium.

(More knocking)

MINA

Who is it?

BILLINGTON

It's Billington, Mum.

(Mina runs to the door...)

MINA

Oh, Billington. It's Lucy. She's taken ill.

BILLINGTON

I heard the bell and wondered if I might be of assistance.

MINA

Yes, please, Billington. Go and fetch Mrs. Westenra.

BILLINGTON

Right away.

(He exits briskly.)

MINA

Dr. Seward! Dr. Seward! Come quickly! It's Lucy!

(She closes the door and goes back to Lucy.)

MINA

I don't know if he hears me. I'll have to run 'cross the lawn. Hold on, Dear. I'll return presently.

(Mina runs out quickly to fetch Dr. Seward. A mysterious music eases in and lights gradually crossfade to a glowing crimson. Lucy, sweating and pallid brings herself up to a sitting position, she moves to the foot of the bed on her knees. The following speech is delivered upright from her bed. Lucy looks out as if seeing and feeling all that she describes.)

LUCY

Yes,… Yesssss,… I hear you, Master. I see it. All. I reach the summit of East Cliff. Gazing below, I spy waves rise in growing fury, each overtopping its fellow. The mysterious glassy seas are like a roaring and devouring monster. White crested waves beat madly on the craggy rock at the foot of the shelving cliff; The wind roars like thundering masses of sea creatures come drifting inland, white wet clouds which sweep by in ghostly fashion so dank and damp and cold that the spirits of those lost at sea were touching my naked body with their clammy hands of death. I so want to join them! I inch closer to the ledge. Compelled to leap off the cliff and dive down to sweet oblivion. And just at the last, before I leap, crushing skull against the rocks below, I spy the corpses of hundreds of souls taken their own lives. The stench of their rotting flesh wafts upward and excites me. Blood-bloated with sickly hue of algae, the dead begin to move, to swim out to deeper ocean and my mouth waters. I desire, I hunger, I THIRST!

(As music dies and lights restore gradually, Lucy appears to come out from under her odd spell. Mina enters hurriedly.)

MINA

He's coming, my sweet.

LUCY

Water, please.

MINA

Yes, yes of course!

(Mina pours a glass of water from a nearby pitcher and takes it to Lucy.)

MINA

Here you are, love.

(Seward enters followed by Hennessey and Snelling.)

SEWARD

What is it?

MINA

It's Lucy, Sir. She's stricken with some fever, I fear.

SEWARD

Oh, Good Lord! Her skin!

(Seward goes to Lucy's bedside. He examines her eyes, mouth, and pulse.)

MINA

It's just come on. She was fine last night.

(Seward notices the two wounds on her neck.)

SEWARD

And these marks? Good God, what's happened to her?

MINA

She was sleep-walking again. I went out to find her. Closing her shawl, I may have caught her in the neck with a safety pin.

SEWARD

Twice?! And so deep into the flesh. No safety pin did this. You can rest easy, Miss Murray. No fault of your own. No, these appear to be wounds from some animal's teeth marks. Fangs. A wolf or something.

MINA

A wolf?! But how could that have happened? She was within my sight most of the time.

SEWARD

Miss Murray, quickly! Come 'round to the other side of the bed and talk to her. Keep her awake. She needs to stay conscious.

MINA

All right… Lucy, it's me, Mina. I'm here.
Everything's going to be all right…

SEWARD

Miss Hennessey, some compresses with a
basin of cold water, if you please.

HENNESSEY

Right away, Doctor.

SEWARD

Smollet, you'd better go and fetch her mother. But don't alarm her. Simply tell her to come to Lucy's bedchamber.

(Enter Mrs. Westenra at the door with Billington.)

SNELLING

It seems she's already here, Dr. Seward.

(Seward runs to stop Mrs. Westenra at the door.)

WESTENRA

What in God's name is happening?! I heard the bell. And some commotion.

SEWARD

Relax, Mrs. Westenra. Everything's in hand. Lucy appears to be a little dehydrated is all.

WESTENRA

I want to see her.

SEWARD

Stay calm. You may see her so long as you don't cause alarm in her.

WESTENRA

Let me see my daughter!

SEWARD

All right but for God's sake, Madam, choose your words carefully. Use diplomacy, Mrs. Westenra. Don't let on how grave she appears. We don't want to worry her unnecessarily. Whatever you do, be gentle.

WESTENRA

Out of my way, Doctor Seward. I know how
to speak to my own daughter.

SEWARD

Very well. And remember your heart condition.
It does you no good to get upset, either.

WESTENRA

(Completely in shock.)

Oh my word, Lucy! You look simply God awful! Why, she's like a dying invalid in the throws of apoplexy! Dear, you're colorless as a decaying corpse, rotting in a charnel house!!!

SEWARD

Your sensitivity is eloquent as always, Madam.

WESTENRA

Well, I'm sorry, Dr. Seward, but just look at her!

SEWARD

I SEE her!

WESTENRA

What in God's name has happened to my baby?!

SEWARD

It appears to be some type of blood poisoning or rather an anemia of sorts that I've not witnessed in my years.

WESTENRA

Dr. Seward, haven't you any smelling salts?

SEWARD

Smelling salts won't help your daughter maintain consciousness.

WESTENRA

Not for her! For me! I'm feeling a hot flash just now.

(She collapses on a chair, waving her face with a fan.)

SEWARD

Miss Snelling, see to Mrs. Westenra. Get her a glass of water.

SNELLING

Yes, Doctor.

SEWARD

Ladies, help Miss Lucy into the water closet. Prepare a cold bath.
Anything to bring her temperature down!

MINA

Dr. Seward, what more can we do? Please,
tell me Lucy's going to be all right.

SEWARD

Miss Murray, this is unfortunately beyond my scope of practice. I
have a very dear friend. My mentor and advisor at School of Medicine.
Professor Abraham Van Helsing of Holland. He'll know what to do.
I'll send a telegram straightaway to Amsterdam! Meanwhile, stay by
her side. Help Mrs. Westenra to more comfortable accommodation.

MINA

Yes, yes, of course.

(Mina and others help Lucy offstage, presumably to a cold bath.)

SEWARD

(Aside. Music in.)

All grows despairing when the Grim Reaper's sickle is brandished.
I fear a battle is eminent against the stranger at death's door.

For Lucy's fever and her mother's failing heart portend darker days upon us. Lord grant that we have responded in time.

(Lights fade. Exeunt.)

END OF ACT I

ACT II

Scene Breakdown

(10-Minute Intermission)

Scene 1

"An Angel of Mercy"

[Whitby, The Westenra Cottage]

(Lights and low, calm underscore accompanies the entrance of Seward followed by Van Helsing. They are just outside Westenra Cottage.)

<u>SEWARD</u>

…and having said that, Professor Van Helsing, I feel she is in need of some sort of phlebotemal treatment. I couldn't very well conduct such a procedure without proper council.

<u>VAN HELSING</u>

Not to vorry, my good friend. When I received your telegram, I vas out the door and on my way. The description of the marks upon her neck has me concerned. Did you adorn ze room with garlic as instructed?

<u>SEWARD</u>

Indeed, Sir, we have. Much to the chagrin of everyone concerned I had our nursing staff hang garlands of the stuff all about. We must've procured every clove in the area.

<u>VAN HELSING</u>

Goot! I must see her immediately.

SEWARD

Come, Professor. The cottage is this way.

VAN HELSING

You left her alone?

SEWARD

Not entirely. A couple of nurses, her mother, and her dear friend, Mina, keep constant vigil. A footman is nearby and friends just outside the door.

VAN HELSING

Have you procured the instruments I requested?

SEWARD

Yes, a trocar, lancet, sterile needles, and transfusion system.

VAN HELSING

Very goot.

SEWARD

So have you a conjecture?

VAN HELSING

I have, for myself, a thought at present. Later, I shall unfold for you.

SEWARD

Why not now? It may do some good; we might arrive at some immediate correct decision.

VAN HELSING

When the time is right. My friend, Jack. We learn from failure. Not from success. We must get it wrong, before we get it right.

SEWARD

This way, Professor.

(Suddenly Dracula appears. A foggy haze surrounds him as he scales a gable atop Whitby cottage. The vampire waves a hand across the men on the ground. They come to a freeze in mid-conversation. Slow music of suspenseful nature underscores the following.)

DRACULA

A visitor! How quaint. But, beware my presence, Dutchman. I came to England to invade a new land. Where, perhaps, for centuries to come I might, amongst its teeming millions, satiate my lust for blood, spread contagion, and create a new and ever-widening circle of semi-demons to batten upon the helpless. My labor has only begun. The measure of leaving my own land, barren of the living, and coming to a new continent where life of man teems till they are as a multitude of standing corn, was the work of centuries. The glimpse I have had of your living world, has only whet my appetite for more, grown my desire. And I am famished. Were another of the Un-Dead, like me, try to do what I have done, not all the centuries of the world would provide sufficient time. And hunters of the vampire?

I will not fear you! For I am the *Wolf* ! Your 'man-eater', as they of Gypsy camps call the werewolf, who has at last, tasted blood of the nineteenth century. As for Miss Lucy? I put my disease in her. Infected her with my poison. None of you are safe as long as I reign supreme in the darkness. 'As flies to wanton boys, I kill you for my sport.' But I shall never die. I come again, and again, and again.

(Dracula waves his hand, he vanishes and the two men are once again animate. They have no idea they had been rendered into suspended animation. They arrive at the steps of the front door. They encounter Holmwood and Morris.)

VAN HELSING
Gentlemen.

SEWARD
Professor Van Helsing, may I introduce the Honorable Arthur Holmwood, the groom-to-be and son of the Lord Godalming.

VAN HELSING
Sir Holmwood? It is a pleasure.

HOLMWOOD
Please, call me 'Arthur'.

VAN HELSING
All right,… Arthur.

HOLMWOOD

Thank you for coming.

SEWARD

And this is Mr. Quincey Morris.

MORRIS

How do, Doc?

VAN HELSING

Charming.

SEWARD

Miss Snelling, our nurse.

(Snelling curtsies.)

SEWARD

Mrs. Westenra, the patient's mother.

(Mrs. Westenra offers her hand.)

MRS. WESTENRA

It is an honor to make your acquaintance, Professor Van Helsing.

VAN HELSING

Madame, the pleasure is all mine.

(He kisses her hand as a gentleman would.)

MRS. WESTENRA

Now, please. See to my Lucy.

(He steps further in)

SEWARD

And this is Nurse Hennessey.

(She curtsies.)

VAN HELSING

Nurse Hennessey.

(He sees Lucy motionless in her bed. He is suddenly alarmed.)

VAN HELSING

Why she's not even conscious!

SEWARD

I thought I conveyed that to you at the train station!

VAN HELSING

I must've misunderstood!

(Van Helsing goes immediately to check her pulse.)

VAN HELSING

It is not too late. Quickly! We'll need two small glasses. One with vater, the other with brandy. And a small cloth for dipping.

(Van Helsing checks under her eyelids.)

HENNESSEY

Right away, Professor.

SEWARD

What can we do?

VAN HELSING

Her skin needs enrichment. It is parched. If we can daub her regularly with the fluid I suggest, it may help to resuscitate.

(Van Helsing takes his stethoscope and listens to her heart.)

SEWARD

Well?

VAN HELSING

Veak heartbeat. She'll need an immediate adrynal injection.

(Van Helsing prepares it. At this time Maid Snelling has brought the small glass of water, and Nurse Hennessey brings the small glass of brandy with cloth. Snelling hands the water to Van Helsing. Hennessey holds the glass of brandy close to the patient and it appears she is going to daub Lucy's skin with the alcohol.)

HENNESSEY

Here's the glass of Brandy, sir. Shall I dab it
on her neck wounds for antiseptic?

VAN HELSING

No, no, no. The vater is for Miss Lucy's
forehead. The brandy is for me.

*(Snelling and Hennessey trade places, Van Helsing downs the shot of
brandy in one fell swoop. Hennessey goes to daub Lucy's head with
the cool, damp cloth.)*

VAN HELSING

I have made a cursory examination and
there is no functional cause.

(Van Helsing gives the injection of adrenaline.)

HOLMWOOD

Cursory?! What does that mean?!

VAN HELSING

All mysteries are contained in the color of her skin.

SEWARD

What can you glean from that?

VAN HELSING

It is the difference between anemia and jaundice. If the skin pallor is an overall light yellow, we may have an anemic condition. If it is stained or splotchy and present in the eyes, it may be jaundice.

(Van Helsing takes a scalpel from Seward, makes a tiny cut in one of Lucy's fingers, takes a drop of her blood, and spreads it on a strange herb from his bag. He smells it, breathing in deeply. He folds it into a small square. He then places the packet upon a small burning candle and the thing goes up suddenly in a puff of smoke and fire. The flame startles everyone.)

VAN HELSING

In this case, it is neither. A shortness of bile. Red
blood cells and iron are in depletion.

HOLMWOOD

Just look at that! We can't trust this man with Lucy's health.

VAN HELSING

Vy? Because I am a philosopher? A metaphysician?
I believe in alchemy and ritual?

SEWARD

Arthur, relax. Professor Van Helsing is also a scientist.

VAN HELSING

I vant more garlic in the room!

HOLMWOOD

He's a madman.

VAN HELSING

Ve are in a phase of spiritual pathology. She must be protected from evil that which it would otherwise harm by contact.

HOLMWOOD

A Bloody Witchdoctor!

SEWARD

(To Morris.)

Get him out of here! I'll not have my friend and mentor insulted!

VAN HELSING

Easy, easy friend Jack. It's all right. He means no harm and no offense taken. It's true, my methods are unorthodox to some, completely insane to many. (To Seward.) Vy don't you go back to your office and rest a while. You've been under considerable strain. I'm alright here.

SEWARD

Very well.

(Exits.)

HOLMWOOD

We hardly know this man!

VAN HELSING

There's time enough later for us to fall in love. Now, if you vill all follow my exact instructions. We'll begin with a blood transfusion of her entire circulatory system.

(Van Helsing begins to set up the instruments and transfusion contraption.)

MORRIS

What are those things?

VAN HESLING

This is the ghastly paraphernalia of our trade. Standard equipment, Mr. Morris. Now, a brave man's blood is the best thing on this earth vhen a woman is in trouble. You're a man and no mistake. Vell, the Devil may work against us for all he's worth, but God sends us men when we need them.

(Van Helsing holds up a hypodermic needle with a long tube connected to it. He rubs alcohol with a cotton ball over the needle.)

Mr. Holmwood, rest easy. It's Lucy must
receive the pinprick. Not you.

HOLMWOOD

What can *I* do? Tell me, and I shall do it. My life is hers. But since, as you said, you'll not be needing to stick that thing in me,... just know that I'd gladly do it. I would give the last drop of blood in my body for her.

VAN HELSING

The last drop? Really?

MORRIS

That's what he said.

VAN HELSING

(To Holmwood.)
Roll up your sleeve.

HOLMWOOD

What?!

VAN HELSING

Blood transfusion. Now!

HOLMWOOD

I thought you said…

VAN HELSING

I lied. Roll up your sleeve. I did say 'a brave man', yes, that's true. But you'll do. Now give us a vein!

(By this point Van Helsing has already placed one end of the tube with needle in Lucy's arm, and now after a brief swabbing of alcohol, does the same into Holmwood's arm. It is quick.)

VAN HELSING

He is so young and strong and of blood so pure that we need not defribinate it. Science, Mr. Holmwood.

HOLMWOOD

More like science fiction.

VAN HELSING

Young man, I am a purveyor of the 'healing craft'. Not just medicine, but the harnessed energies of mother earth, the cosmos, the universe. *(Finishes with insertion of transfusion tubes.)* There, that should do it.

(Enter Hawkins.)

HAWKINS

Professor Van Helsing?

VAN HELSING

Ja? Vat is it, young man?

HAWKINS

I'm Hawkins. The Westenra's footman.
May I have a word in private, Sir?

VAN HELSING

For a moment, certainly. *(To Holmwood)* Careful
not to jostle the transfusion tubes.

(They cross away from the others in order to have a private conversation. Hawkins removes a telegram from his waistcoat.)

VAN HELSING

Now, vat can I do for you, good Mr. Hawkins?

HAWKINS

It's a telegram, sir. It was wired into Dr. Seward's office just half an hour ago. He said to deliver it to you and let you decide what's to be done. Addressed to "The Honorable Arthur Holmwood", hereafter "The Lord Godalming".

VAN HELSING

Vat? Let me read that. Mein Gott! His father has died. Arthur is now the *Lord Godalming.* Inheritor of his father's estate and title.

HAWKINS

Dr. Seward felt that you may not want him
to receive the news at this time.

VAN HELSING

Jack Seward is prudent. Keep this confidential. I will inform Arthur later this evening. It is certain he will desire a train post-haste to make his father's funeral. He'll be away for several days. Have Seward's office arrange the travel fare.

HAWKINS

Yes, Professor.

(Hawkins exits, Van Helsing pockets the telegram and crosses back to those tending on Lucy.)

VAN HELSING

Arthur, gently carry Lucille to the water closet. There the nurses will give her a cool bath to lower her temperature. Now everyone! To your work!

*(Suspenseful music in as everyone exits
and lights fade on the boudoir.)*

VAN HELSING

With such advancement comes such sorrow.

[END OF SCENE]

Scene 2

"Hoard of the Flies"

[Whitby Asylum]

*(Enter Dr. Seward and Waites Simmons who
is carrying an empty canary cage.)*

<u>SEWARD</u>

What is it, Simmons?

<u>SIMMONS</u>

My canary, Guvna. She's been missing from her cage since sun-up.
I've me suspicion, but I'll be dogged if I can reckon out how that
loony bugger escaped from his cell.

<u>SEWARD</u>

All right, Mr. Simmons. Bring him here. We'll inquire as to the
whereabouts of your bird and see if we can sort this out.

<u>SIMMONS</u>

Right then, Guvna. All right, now, Mr. Renfield. Come along. Dr.
Seward would like to have a word with you.

(Simmons pulls Renfield out of his cell.)

SEWARD

Mr. Renfield, it has come to my attention that Mr. Waites Simmons' pet bird has gone missing from its cage. What do you know about this?

(Renfield simply shrugs, but says nothing as his mouth is full.)

SEWARD

Speak up, Mr. Renfield. Do you know anything regarding the whereabouts of Mr. Simmons canary? Come on, man. Out with it!

(At this, Renfield can retain his silence no longer as he had been holding his breath from the start. He chokes and blows a flurry of yellow feathers out of his mouth. They float to the floor like a bizarre snow of flaxen.)

RENFIELD

No, good Doctor. Renfield wouldn't know
what happened to the little critter.

SIMMONS

Blimey… He ate my canary!

SEWARD

MR. RENFIELD!!! You ate Mr. Simmons'
canary? How could you do it?

RENFIELD

With a tablespoon of malt vinegar and a pinch of salt.

SEWARD

I wasn't asking how you prepared the meal. I meant, how could you ingest a poor man's pet?

RENFIELD

Woke up with a craving for fowl, I suppose.

SIMMONS

How dare you!
(The sound of thousands of flies eases in.)

RENFIELD

Do you hear that, Doctor? That unmistakable noise?

SEWARD

Nothing but the sound of a few flies.

RENFIELD

Hoards of buzzing blowflies.

(Renfield produces a large jar packed with blowflies.)

RENFIELD

That's the dinner bell. Renfield is reaping quite a harvest of them.

SIMMONS

Why there must be a million of 'em!

RENFIELD

I once knew a little boy who put so many flies in a bottle that they had no room but to die.

SIMMONS

You can't eat all those!

RENFIELD

I don't intend to, Mr. Simmons. Renfield's going to fatten them up, feed them to a colony of spiders, who when bloated like molasses-filled balloons will burst betwixt his bites like ripened plums. Then he'll feast and he'll feast, and he'll feast!... Doctor, won't you be very good to Renfield and let him have more cubes of sugar? It would do him good.

SIMMONS

And the flies?

RENFIELD

Aye! The flies enjoy it, too! And Renfield fancies the flies. Ergo, Renfield delights in the sweetness.

SEWARD

Very well. I shall procure you a double supply of lumps and leave you as happy man as, I suppose, any in the world. Would that I could fathom your mind.

RENFIELD

To do that, 'oh learned one', you would need to carve open my pate like a pumpkin. You would drive into this melancholy melon, cut open a doorway, then skittle inside like a tarantula. But then, irony of ironies, you'd no longer be the examiner. You would be cursed by madness from within. Would you suffocate, Doctor Seward, within the walls of this skull? Or would you, like the very larvae infecting said grey matter, thrive?

(Seward opens his mouth to reply but cannot find an appropriate response.)

RENFIELD

Squiggle and squirm, like carnivorous worm,
Breeding disease as good as you please?
Or
Like black widows in pockets,
Crawl out of eye sockets?

SEWARD

Well, it's been quite the encounter, Mr.
Renfield. We'll see you tomorrow.

SIMMONS

Not if I can help it.

SEWARD

Now, now, Simmons. Let's be charitable.
We'll replace your canary, forthwith.

SIMMONS

Come along, ye foul eater of fowl.

(Simmons leads Renfield by the chain attached to his collar. Foreboding music eases in and Renfield slowly turns his head to look in the direction of the Westenra cottage. He halts suddenly.)

RENFIELD

I shall be patient, Master! It is coming! It is coming!

Simmons begins to push him back into the cell. Lights fade on the asylum. Music play on into the next scene.)

[END OF SCENE]

Scene 3

"When the Wolfsbane Blooms"

[Lucy's Boudoir]

(A growing storm with clouds gathering outside. The distant rumbling of thunder followed by lightning. The thunder grows louder and the flashes of lightning outside the gothic windows come more quickly and more often. The light in the bedroom chamber is blue. The blue is broken up at points by the amber glow of flame flickering from candles and lanterns about. Throughout the following scene, thunder crashes more loudly and loudly and lightning flashes more brightly at each explosion of thunder. Lucy sleeps. Her mother enters and is hit by the powerful stench of garlic. This time, she cannot tolerate the smell.)

<u>MRS. WESTENRA</u>

It wreaks in this room! It smells of an Italian brothel.

(Mrs. Westenra removes the necklace from Lucy's neck and then begins ripping down the garlic cloves roped about the windows and doors.)

<u>LUCY</u>

Mother, what are you doing? The professor strictly forbids us all from disturbing the garlic.

MRS. WESTENRA

You're having trouble breathing as it is, Love. You certainly don't need this wrapped about your neck. And all this hanging about? Out with it! Let me crack some windows. It's awfully close in here. I was uneasy about you, darling, and came in to see that you were all right.

LUCY

Close the windows, Mother. Remember your condition. You'll catch your death of cold, Come, take a comforter.

(Mrs. Westenra suddenly catches sight of something outside the French door windows. Forboding music eases in.)

MRS. WESTENRA

Oh Dear Lord.

LUCY

What is it?

(Lucy sits upright in bed.)

MRS. WESTENRA

Out the window on the front lawn. It's a grey wolf! The Gazette spoke of an escaped wolf from the zoo. Do you suppose…?

LUCY

Even if it is the same one, we're all right.

(Mrs. Westenra begins to talk strangely as she has gone into some sort of trance.)

MRS. WESTENRA

No, we're not all right, Lucy.

LUCY

Why do you say that?

MRS. WESTENRA

He's standing upright. On his hind legs. Like a man. It's a werewolf and he has seen me.

LUCY

Mother, please. No more jesting. You're scaring me?

MRS. WESTENRA

It's him. The one who hungers.

LUCY

Mother, what is happening to you?

MRS. WESTENRA

He's speaking to me. Through his eyes.

LUCY

We're at least twenty meters above lawn. We're safe here, Mother.

MRS. WESTENRA

There is no safety, my love. He's floating at the window now.

LUCY

I see nothing, Mother.

MRS. WESTENRA

He's right in front of me, Lucille! He's coming
for me! I'm here, Great One!

*(Music rises to crescendo. Panes of glass from the French window
doors smash inward. Mrs. Westenra, as if by the volition of the
supernatural, bolts to the French window doors, opens them and
leaps out. Lightning, thunder, and music intensifies with the sounds
of a wolf attacking and Mrs. Westenra screaming. Fountains of
crimson blood begin spewing forth from the French door windows.
The grue hits Lucy on face and body until she looks as though she
has just bathed in blood. There is a lighting and music change. Lucy
lies back onto her propped pillows. All this is done to convey the
passage of time. Enter Seward, Van Helsing and a couple of nurses.
The doctors stand at the foot of Lucy's bed as though listening to the
last of Lucy's account. Seward's nurses clean Lucy's face.)*

LUCY

…I tried to pacify her, to no avail. I could hear her poor dear
heart still beating terribly. After a while there was the

low howl again and shortly after there was a crash at the window, and a lot of broken glass was hurled to the floor; scattered shards crystallized the hardwood. The window blinds blew back with the wind that rushed in, and outside the broken panes there was the head of a great, gaunt, grey werewolf! Suddenly, mother lept out of the window and into the lycan's mouth. She cried out in a fright as the sounds of gnashing teeth devoured her.

(Lucy slowly drops her head to her pillow. She appears to have fainted. Van Helsing addresses the nursing staff.)

VAN HELSING

Cool her down with compress. Let her rest but keep her conscious. Close and lock all the windows again. And for God's sake put back the garlic. Over the doors, and the necklace about her throat. Do it! Now!

(Lights fade from Lucy's bed. The nurses do all that is instructed of them to restore what Mrs. Westenra had removed. Van Helsing and Seward turn downstage.)

VAN HELSING

That foolish woman! Right before she died, Mrs. Westenra removed all the garlic and cracked open the windows. It was her. I'm certain of it!

SEWARD

I know, and you know, that Mrs. Westenra had disease of the heart. And we can certify that she died of it. Poor Lucy's account is the result of dementia brought on by fever.

VAN HELSING

Is it?

SEWARD

You don't mean to tell me you believe that story about a werewolf.

VAN HELSING

If this was nothing more than heart failure, then why was she found on the lawn outside the French door windows?

SEWARD

You *do* think this was some sort of werewolf!

VAN HELSING

I don't know. We'll have to examine the body. Come along.

SEWARD

We can't do that now. Scotland Yard has just arrived. You saw them as we got to the gate. It's a full inquest. We cannot investigate until the police turn her over to the undertaker.

VAN HELSING

Well then, we wait. Come, let us observe.

(Exeunt)

[END OF SCENE]

Scene 4

"A Seeming Deathbed"

[Lucy's Boudoir]

(Music in. Lighting rises on Lucy's bedchamber. Holmwood sleeps on a couch nearby. Morris is dozing off in a seated position on a chair. Smollet Snelling, one of the nurses, is placing cool compresses on Lucy's forehead. Van Helsing enters followed by Seward. They go straight to the bed to examine their patient.)

<u>VAN HELSING</u>
Dr. Seward, look at her mouth.

<u>SEWARD</u>
It must be some trick of the light. Her canine teeth look longer and sharper than all the rest.

*(Suddenly, ther is a loud and strange sound
just outside the French door windows.)*

<u>VAN HELSING</u>
Vat on earth is that?

<u>SEWARD</u>
It sounds like some slapping or buffeting
at the window… I'll investigate.

(He goes toward the window.)

SNELLING

Don't go over there, Doctor.

SEWARD

Never you worry, Smollet. Good Lord!

VAN HELSING

What is it? What do you see, Jack?

SEWARD

In the full moonlight I can see… Oh dear! It is a great bat! Wheeling round and round. Doubtless attracted by the light from within Lucy's bedchamber. It's striking the window panes with its wings as though trying to force its way in!

VAN HELSING

Away from the window, Dr. Seward! Go over there and wake that poor man. *(Gentle music in, underscoring the rest of the scene.)* Let him come and see the last. He trusts us and we have promised him.

(Seward wakes Holmwood. Morris stirs as well. The three men join Van Helsing at Lucy's side.

VAN HELSING

Come, come good Arthur. Take her hand
in yours. But do not kiss her.

(Holmwood does so.)

HOLMWOOD

She is cold. Cold as a stone.

SEWARD

(Checking vitals)

It's all over now. It is done. She is dead.

(Quincy and Holmwood and any nurses nearby all kneel down at Lucy's side and pray for her soul. Van Helsing pulls Seward away for a moment.)

SEWARD

Poor girl. There is peace for her at last. It is the end.

VAN HELSING

Not so, alas, not so. Would it were true. Jack,
my friend, this is only the beginning.

(They join the others at Lucy's bedside. If necessary in the production, she can be lifted by all and carried off carefully and somberly off the stage. Everyone would then exit with her.)

[END OF SCENE]

Scene 5

"Post Mortem"

[The Undertaker's Parlor]

(In funereal music, Mr. Swales, Smollet Snelling, Patti Hennesey, Waites Simmons, and Mildred Creaply, the undertaker's wife, prepare a funeral parlor for viewing. Two open caskets are wheeled in; One holds Lucy's body, the other Mrs. Westenra. Tributes, wreathes, and flowers are placed in various areas. Last minute powdering is applied to the corpses' faces by Mrs. Creaply. All five staff members simultaneously tend to the ghastly preparations as the audience observes the subtle scene change. This should all be quick, yet done with reverence and care. Dr. Seward enters. Swales, Snelling, Hennesey, and Simmons exit. Mrs. Creaply approaches Seward.)

CREAPLY

She makes quite a beautiful corpse, don't she, guvna? Just lovely. I mean, the girl. Not her mum. It's been my privilege to attend upon young Lucille. Its not too much to say that she will set quite an example of superior craftsmanship by our establishment.

SEWARD
Indeed, Mrs. Creaply. She looks almost human.
You are a credit to your profession.

CREAPLY
Thank you, Sir.

SEWARD

And the obsequies?

CREAPLY

The funeral is arranged for tomorrow, Doctor. So that the poor girl and her mum might be buried together… That is to say, at the same *time*. Not in the same receptacle, of course.

SEWARD

Yes, *that* I was able to intuit. Now, as for
the bodies, how do they stand?

CREAPLY

Oh there's no standin', Sir. They've both gone quite beyond that. Them bein' deceased and all. However, I do know a photographer who props up his clients for tin-types, post-rigor, for family mementos. Did you want us to insert rods and such into their…

SEWARD

I MEANT,… *(more calmly)*… When I asked how the bodies "stood", I was referring to your preparations for burial!

CREAPLY

Oh dear me! So sorry, guvna'. I'm all finished.
All but the posies for their sachets.

SEWARD

Well, see to it, straightaway.

CREAPLY

Very good, Sir.

(Mrs. Creaply begins to exit just as Van Helsing enters.)

VAN HELSING

No need, Mrs. Creaply. I've taken the liberty of providing the posies myself. Doctor Seward's staff will continue with the preparations presently. Go somewhere, lie down, and rest yourself.

CREAPLY

Very well, Professor.

(She exits. As soon as Van Helsing is sure he and the doctor are alone, he speaks to Seward in a conspiratorial voice.)

VAN HELSING

Tomorrow before night, I want you to bring
me a post-mortem bone saw.

SEWARD

Must we perform an autopsy?

VAN HELSING

Yes, and no. I want to operate, but not as you think. Let me tell you now, bug not a word to another. I need to perform a type of procedure upon Miss Lucy's body.

SEWARD

But why? The girl is dead. Why practice upon her without purpose? To do so is monstrous!

VAN HELSING

Friend Jack. There are things that you know not, but that you shall know and bless me for knowing, though they be most unpleasant. There are strange and terrible days before us. Let us not be two, but one, so that we can work to a good end. Will you not have faith in me?

(Van Helsing extends his hand. Seward takes it and returns a firm grip of solidarity.)

SEWARD

I give you my promise. Now, what do you propose?

VAN HELSING

A private matter that must be kept secret from the would-be bride-groom. If, however, Arthur should become wise, tell him that I will execute a relatively simple procedure. Assure him it is both respectful to her corpse and quite non-invasive.

SEWARD

And that is?

VAN HELSING

I want to chop off her head and cut out her heart.
(Music. In shock, Seward exits disgustedly. Van Helsing claps his hands together twice to summon Swales, Snelling,

Hennessey, and Simmons. The three enter with hat boxes filled with garlic strands, wreathes, and single cloves. Van Helsing digs into his waistcoat and pulls out several pound notes. He pays each one of them off. He exits as the three completely and quickly festoon the parlor with garlic. They exit briskly.)

[END OF SCENE]

Scene 6

"It Is The Man Himself!"

[Garden Cemetery, Whitby]

*(Pleasant music as Jonathan and Mina enter
to stroll through the garden cemetery)*

<u>MINA</u>

The day is so beautiful, yet so clouded with mourning. I simply can't stop thinking of those I love, now lost.

<u>HARKER</u>

I had hoped our walks throughout Whitby would do us good. You know, get our minds off things. If only for a while.

<u>MINA</u>

It's a sweet thought, my love.

<u>HARKER</u>

Sweet thoughts, yet little difference they make, I suppose.

(They sit together on a bench.)

<u>MINA</u>

Its only, there's hardly a curative for the grief-stricken. What with the deaths of so many within our circle. Only time will heal wounds of the heart.

HARKER

Mina, remember when we were young? I mean younger. Our parents must've thought we were absolutely mad. For hardly a fortnight passed that we didn't sneak into the gardens of the others' homes and climb the trellises as in "Romeo and Juliet".

MINA

Yes! I *do* remember! How joyous, our youth! Oh, Jonathan. Hold me by the arm. The way you used to in days of old, before I went to school.

(He does so.)

HARKER

How's this, Love?

MINA

Much better.

HARKER

See if *this* is much better.

(Jonathan steals a quick kiss from Mina's lips.)

MINA

OH! Jonathan! How cheeky! And I, a pedant of etiquette, manners, and decorum for young ladies. I shall be banished from her majesty's kingdom of polite and civilized society. For some don't even hold hands in public 'till after their third child.

HARKER

I don't think anyone saw us.

MINA

You know something? I don't care if they did.
You are my husband, I am your wife.

(Mina now initiates a kiss. Jump scare chord. Dracula appears in one area of the garden. Jonathan sees him and he bolts upright off the bench. Dracula vanishes.)

HARKER

My God!

MINA

What is it, Jonathan?

HARKER

Look! Over there! Did you not see it?!

MINA

What?

(Dracula appears again, this time at a completely different area far way from the first. This appearing and reappearing at different locations can be done through the use of a

double. The impression of course should be that the vampire is quickly transporting himself supernaturally from one place to the other.)

HARKER

There he is again!

(Dracula vanishes.)

HARKER

Look now! He's gone!

MINA

What was it that disturbed you so?

HARKER

I gazed at a tall, thin man with a beaked nose and black moustache, pointed beard. His face was not a good face. It was hard, cruel, and sensual. His large white teeth looked all the whiter because his lips were blood-red. His teeth were pointed like that of a wolf. Can't you understand who it was?

(Dracula appears somewhere else.)

HARKER

Do you see who it is?

(Dracula vanishes.)

MINA

No, Dear, I don't see anyone. Who is it?

HARKER

It is the man himself!

MINA

Who? Tell me, who?!

(Dracula appears again.)

HARKER

He appears! He vanishes!

(Again he's gone.)

MINA

Where?

HARKER

I just saw him over there. And then, then he reappeared there. And then here!

(Dracula appears, then disappears.)

HARKER

And there!

MINA

Oh my dear, dear husband. You *are* mad.

HARKER

He's toying with me.

MINA

You are infirm with nerves.

HARKER

He's here, Mina. And what's more… He wants us to know it.

MINA

You're scaring me. You've lost reality.

HARKER

No, I assure you. I am very much replete with sanity.

MINA

I'm not comfortable here, all of a sudden.

HARKER

Nor I. Come, Mina. This place is not safe.

(Music of suspense. Husband and wife exit the garden. The same music leads into the next scene.)

[END OF SCENE]

Scene 7

"Revelations"

[Seward's Office, Whitby Asylum]

(Enter Van Helsing, followed by Seward.)

<u>VAN HELSING</u>

You need not trouble with the bone saw. We will not do it.

<u>SEWARD</u>

Why not? Only three nights ago you were so resolute.

<u>VAN HELSING</u>

Because it is too late.

(The professor hands a copy of the Morning Gazette to the Doctor.)

What do you think of that?

(Seward gives the paper a cursory glance.)

<u>SEWARD</u>

I don't know what you mean.

<u>VAN HELSING</u>

Here, beneath this headline…

(Seward reads aloud.)

SEWARD

"At the cliffs near Whitby Abbey, innocent children are being lured away, evidently decoyed by a mysterious woman yet to be identified. When the children are recovered, it is discovered they all share identical sets of marks. Pairs of deep puncture wounds are bored into their throats."

VAN HELSING

Well?

SEWARD

It's like poor Lucy's.

VAN HELSING

And what do you make of it?

SEWARD

Simply that there is some cause in common. Whatever it was that injured her, has injured them.

VAN HELSING

That is true indirectly, but not directly.

SEWARD

How do you mean, Professor? Tell me. I can hazard no opinion. I do not know what to think and I have no data upon which to found a conjecture.

VAN HELSING

Do you mean to tell me, friend Jack, that you have no suspicion as to what Lucille Westenra died of? Not after all the clues given. Not only by events but by me?

SEWARD

Of nervous prostration. Followed by a great loss or waste of blood.

VAN HELSING

And how the blood lost or waste?

SEWARD

I know not. That I cannot decipher.

VAN HELSING

You are a clever man, Jack. You reason well and your wit is bold. Listen to me. In some islands of the Western seas, bats hunt at night and the very sailors who sleep on the decks of their ships, in the morning are found dead men. White, even as Miss Lucy was? And there are some human-like creatures who cannot die.

SEWARD

I am bewildered by such ideas.

VAN HELSING

Can you say with absolute conviction that Lucy is now, even as we speak, sealed in her crypt?

SEWARD

With absolute certainty? No. For I never observed Mr. Swales perform the interment.

VAN HELSING

Let's imagine he did. Yet what if Lucy herself has become... a vampire.

SEWARD

What!

VAN HELSING

I want you to believe.

SEWARD

Believe in what, exactly?

VAN HELSING

In things that your reason tells you, you should not believe... Come with me.

SEWARD

Where are we going?

VAN HELSING

You're going to take me to the cell of one, R. M. Renfield. Your man, Mr. Simmons just found me in the hallway. He told me that this man urgently wants to speak with me and Miss Mina as well. Mina is also very concerned it seems with mental disturbances in her husband, Jonathan. Let's find Mina and to Renfield's cell.

SEWARD

This way, Professor!

(Exeunt.)

[END OF SCENE]

Scene 8
"Warning and Betrayal"

Renfield's cell, Whitby Asylum

(Music. Renfield's cellblock. Enter Seward,
Mina, and Van Helsing...)

SEWARD

All right, Renfield. We've summoned Mrs. Harker and Professor Van Helsing. Say what you have to say and do it with speed.

RENFIELD

Rats! Rats! Rats! Hundreds, thousands, millions of them! And every one a life! I hunger for rats now. And soon I shall hunger for larger, living things!

SEWARD

More delusions? Right then, we'll be on our way. Come, friends.

VAN HELSING

Just a moment, Doctor. Mr. Renfield, I am Professor Van Helsing.

RENFIELD

I know exactly who you are.

VAN HELSING
You wanted to see me?

RENFIELD
Aye, to ask you to be Mrs. Harker's protector.

MINA
Protect me from what?

RENFIELD
Where are you staying?

MINA
At the Westenra cottage adjacent to the old abbey.

RENFIELD
Oh! Stay not there!

MINA
But, why not?

RENFIELD
It isn't safe.

MINA
Why?

RENFIELD

The blood! The blood is the life! And now yours is in jeopardy.

MINA

By what? By whom?

RENFIELD

Dr. Seward, in the name of all that is holy, protect this dear woman from the fiend. He is my master and I obey him, but just this once, I must warn Mrs. Harker to lock herself up. Stay in hiding with your husband, Jonathan. If not, the same fate of Miss Lucy will befall you!

MINA

What fate is it you speak of, Mr. Renfield?

RENFIELD

The Professor knows. Don't you? He can tell you. You've no doubt heard of the "Bloofer Lady"? My master is lord of all vampires, Count Dracula! Miss Lucy is now un-dead, his concubine. He has bitten her. She now bites the children.

SEWARD

The "Bloofer Lady"! But Mr. Renfield, where does this name come from? Why do the children refer to her this way?

RENFIELD

Because Miss Lucy is beautiful, still. At least to the children. And when they try to pronounce the word, 'beautiful', it comes out 'bloofer'. Mrs. Harker, I implore you to stay here in the Asylum. It is the safest place!

VAN HELSING

Though this sounds of madness, there is method in it. Seward, can you accommodate Mr. and Mrs. Harker at your asylum?

SEWARD

I can. We have a small room with a bed we can use for guests. Mrs. Harker, step outside the door for a moment. When we finish here, we'll escort you to a safe room.

MINA

Yes, Doctor.

(She leaves.)

RENFIELD

Let me entreat you, Dr. Seward, oh, let me implore you, to let me out of this asylum at once! And do it secretly, in daylight. Send me away how you will and where you will; send keepers with me, bearing whips and chains; Let them take me in a straight waistcoat, manacled, and leg-ironed, even to a jail, but let me go out of this!

VAN HELSING

Come with me, Dr. Seward. We must make plans. And we must share them with the others. We'll need all the help we can get. I'll explain it all to you. For there is an evil burning in our midst. And vee are the chosen ones to extinguish the flames!

(Music. The two men exit. Renfield is left
alone in his cell. Fade to black.)

[END OF SCENE]

Scene 9

"Suffer the Children"

A Wooded Area, Whitby

(Mysterious music eases in. Fog rolls about. Blue lighting illuminates the forest area where Dracula appears. Dracula stands motionless and gestures as though conjuring the appearance of the un-dead Lucy Westenra. The "Bloofer Lady", slowly enters as if gliding upon a wisp of smoke. At a given moment in the music, small children appear one by one from behind trees, between shrubs, from the deep woodlands as though stirring from a deep and restful sleep. Like a bizarre Pied Piper of Hamlin, the "Bloofer Lady" beckons the children with her hands to follow her. Slowly, in a daze-like state, zombie-like, they walk up to her and each child clutches hold of part of her gown, cape, and/or train. Dracula approaches her, they kiss passionately, then she turns to walk towards the woods. The children follow behind her and all vanish among the trees and darkness.)

END OF ACT II

ACT III

Scene Breakdown

Scene 1

"Jack Straw's Castle"

[A Tavern in Exeter]

(Music. Lights come up in a smooth, gradual, and magical glow in the interior of "Jack Straw's Castle", a cozy little tavern. Van Helsing, Godalming (formerly Holmwood), and Morris are revealed seated at a table, eating and drinking. A serving wench brings a bowl of bread, clears a dish or two and then exits. Music fades.)

VAN HELSING
Good food, Ja?

MORRIS
Best chow I've had in a coon's age.

VAN HELSING
It should be. For this is Jack Straw's Castle. The food is hot, the place is warm. The fireplace is always stoked.

GODALMING
Yes, Professor. Very nice. Now, I wish you'd reveal your intention behind this impromptu meeting.

VAN HELSING
Of course. You don't think I brought you here for quaint conversation.

GODALMING
That I doubt.

VAN HELSING
Nor have I brought you here to discuss body fluids, the four humors, open wounds, and dried pools of coagulated blood.

*(He immediately picks up a plate of liver and
holds it under Godalming's nose.)*

More kidney pie?

GODALMING
I believe I'll pass on that for now, Professor.
Now, what's this all about?
*(Van Helsing brings a crowbar out of his leather
bag and places it on the dinner table.)*

MORRIS
What have you got there?

VAN HELSING
An iron crow. Which you English call a 'crow bar'.

GODALMING
We know what it is, Professor. But why have
you brought it to the dinner table?

VAN HELSING

It's for later. To open a crypt.

GODALMING

A crypt. What crypt?

VAN HELSING

There is a grave duty to be done.

GODALMING

What the devil are you talking about, old man?

VAN HELSING

You were, doubtless, surprised by my letter?

GODALMING

I was. It rather upset me for a bit. There has been so much trouble around my house of late, that I could do without a trifle more.

VAN HELSING

Yes, I know. Your father has died. And now
you've a new title, inheritance,...

GODALMING

If you're suggesting that I'm better off without him,... Listen here, old man... I'd rather my father were alive and I a pauper, than to be without him and this title foisted upon me. And his passing so soon upon the heels of losing my fiancé to some malady I've yet to understand.

MORRIS

Out with it, Professor. What's this mission? We're a bit befuddled. 'Cause as it stands now, we don't know our blame hawk from a handsaw.

VAN HELSING

Ah! Ah-Ha! A hand-saw! You are closer than you think!

GODALMING

What do you mean?

VAN HELSING

I want you to come with me, and in secret,
to the churchyard at Kingstead.

GODALMING

Where poor Lucy is buried?

VAN HELSING

Ja.

MORRIS

And once we're there, then what?

VAN HELSING

We enter the tomb.

GODALMING

Professor, are you in earnest or is this some monstrous joke?

MORRIS

And once we're in the tomb?

VAN HELSING

We open the coffin.

GODALMING

For what purpose?!

VAN HELSING

Exhumation.

GODALMING

This is too much! I am willing to be patient in all things that are reasonable; but in this, this desecration of a grave, of one who, …..

VAN HELSING

You will understand when we arrive. If I could spare you one pang, my poor friend, God knows I would. But this night our feet must tread in thorny paths. If not, the feet you love will forever walk in paths of flame!

GODALMING

Take care, Sir, take care!

MORRIS

Easy now, Art. Easy, friend.

VAN HELSING

Lord Godalming, I will reveal all to you! Would it not be well to hear what I have to say?

(After a moment's pause.)

GODALMING

All right. I will listen. That is all I will promise.

VAN HELSING

That is all I ask. If we are finished here, I shall explain all along the way. Come, let us pay for our meal, gentlemen, and be gone. I will alert Dr. Seward to our purposes. Meantime, you two do the same with young Mr. Harker. With the five of us, more crow bars, lanterns, and fresh horses, we should be able to move the stone lid of Miss Lucy's grave. And do what is to be done. Come!

(Exeunt.)

[END OF SCENE]

Scene 2

"Behold the Un-Dead"

[Kingstead]

(Dr. Seward and Jonathan Harker enter Lucy's tomb at Kingstead.)

HARKER

You were right. Kingstead *is* very much an eerie crypt.

SEWARD

Yes, most crypts are.

HARKER

Look. This is indeed the tomb of Lucy Westenra. Her name is carved into the stone.

SEWARD

I told you. I've been here before you know.

HARKER

So you've indicated. I hope we're doing the right thing.

SEWARD

Never you worry. Trust in the Professor
and all things will come to light.

HARKER

Speaking of which, my lantern is very
little help in the darkness here.

SEWARD

It is a profound darkness, of that you can be assured.

HARKER

What on earth could be keeping the other three?

SEWARD

Gathering the necessary supplies. The Professor promised to dole
them out as soon as he arrived.

HARKER

He may want to hurry. I don't know how
long my flame will hold out.

VOICES

It's this way! They've opened the tomb!
Come along! Where's her crypt?

HARKER

In here, Gentlemen!

(Enter Van Helsing, Godalming, and Morris.)

VAN HELSING

Ah! Thank you, young Jonathan. Now, gather round. I've assembled your kits. *(He hands out leather carrying cases)* One for each of you. Open and check your inventory. First, an iron crow, second, two wooden stakes, then a hammer with which to drive them, a vial of Holy water, a strand of garlic, a small prayer book, and most importantly, a crucifix forged in pure silver! You all remember how I taught you to use them, Ja?

HARKER

We do. We've been practicing the rituals.

VAN HELSING

Young Jonathan, we'll not need our prayer books or perform a ceremony. What we have to do is simple. Now, no delay, take your crows and help to crack open her sealed coffin!

(Music in. They do so. And open the lid finding the body of Lucy missing.)

GODALMING

Good Lord! Where is she?! You knew she was gone! What have you done?

VAN HELSING

Dr. Seward, you were with me here yesterday. Was the body of Miss Lucy in that coffin?

SEWARD

It was.

VAN HELSING

You hear? And yet there is one who does not believe with me.

GODALMING

The coffin is empty!

VAN HELSING

It is *now*, Ja! Very observant are you.

(Godalming grabs Van Helsing by the lapels.)

GODALMING

What have you done with her, old man?! Tell me! Or by all that is holy, I'll cast you to such a crypt as this!

*(Morris jumps in between the men and pries
Godalming's hands from Van Helsing.)*

MORRIS

Professor, I answered for you. Your word is all I want. I wouldn't ask such a thing ordinarily. I wouldn't so dishonor you as to imply a doubt; but this is a mystery that goes beyond any honor or dishonor. Is this your doin'?

VAN HELSING

I swear to you by all that I hold sacred that I
have not removed nor touched her!

(Godalming releases. Van Helsing brushes himself off.)

SEWARD

This is what happened: Two nights ago the professor and I came
here – with good purpose, believe me. We opened this coffin, which
was then sealed up, and we found it, as through the trees. Completely
empty! No body at all.

VAN HELSING

And the next day we came here in daytime, and
she lay there. Did she not, friend Jack?

SEWARD

Yes. She did. On mine honor, I can vouch for it. That night we were
just in time. The papers had announced another sighting of the so-
called "Bloofer Lady". One more small child was missing. We found
it, thank God, unharmed amongst the graves.

VAN HELSING

Yesterday I came here before sundown, for
at sundown the Un-Dead can move.

MORRIS

The what?

GODALMING

Un-Dead?

VAN HELSING

Ja. It is a term for that which is neither of this
world nor the underworld beyond.

GODALMING

Is my Lucy alive?

VAN HELSING

(Makes the universal sign with his hand meaning "More or Less")
Ehhhhhhh.

GODALMING

What does *that* mean?!

HARKER

Tell us more.

VAN HELSING

I waited here all the night till the sun rose, but I saw nothing. It was
most probable that it was because I had laid over the clamps of those
doors, garlic, which the vampire, or Un-Dead, cannot bear, and other
things which they shun. Last night there was no exodus, so tonight
before the sundown I took away my garlic and other things. And so it
is, we find this coffin empty. But bear with me. So far there is

much that is strange. Wait you with me within, unseen and unheard, and things much stranger are yet to be.

GODALMING

I simply cannot believe that this, this so-called "Bloofer Lady", this child ravager is the work of my poor deceased Lucy!

VAN HELSING

Believe it, Arthur.

HARKER

I have several times encountered Count Dracula, the vampire king. I know it all to be true.

VAN HELSING

I am keeping the tomb open. So that the Un-Dead may return.

MORRIS

And is that stuff you have put there going to do it?

VAN HELSING

Always does.

GODALMING

Great Scott! What sort of game are you playing, Van Helsing?

VAN HELSING

It is no game, I assure you, Lord Godalming.

GODALMING

What is that?

VAN HELSING

The host. I brought it from Amsterdam. It is
the Holy wafer. I have an indulgence.

(Lighting change, music in, a strange sound and smoke billows in bringing with it the vampire, Lucy!)

HARKER

Make haste, gentlemen! The thing arrives!

VAN HELSING

Hide yourselves!

(Lucy enters in the red velvet wedding dress within which she was buried. She glides in amongst red smoke and fog. She is clearly a full-fledged vampire, newly un-dead. She carries a small living boy with her.)

GODALMING

It is her face.

HARKER

And yet how changed!

GODALMING

Good Lord! She's carrying someone's child!

SEWARD

Her sweetness has turned to adamantine, heartless cruelty.

MORRIS

Her lips are crimson with fresh blood.

GODALMING

What was it that stained the purity of her death-robe?

HARKER

Van Helsing, your iron nerve is failing?

VAN HELSING

No. It is a *thing*.

MORRIS

It bears her shape, yet it is nothing more than a thing.

VAN HELSING

And the babe is her feast. We must save the boy…

(Van Helsing leaps out from his hiding spot and waves his torch. This distracts Lucy who drops the boy. The boy escapes, running out of the tomb. Lucy hisses at Van Helsing, till she sees Godalming.)

LUCY

Come to me, Arthur. Leave these others and come to me. My arms are hungry for you. Come, and we can rest together. Come, my husband, come!

GODALMING

How I miss you!

LUCY

Now, we can be together for all eternity, my Love. Come to me!

(She steps into her own coffin as though crawling into bed to make love to Arthur.)

SEWARD

Arthur, stay back! It is nothing more than an illusion! She is no more your Lucy than an apparition.

VAN HELSING

Shall I move forward, Arthur? Have you seen enough now?

GODALMING

I miss her so.

(Lucy slowly, gradually lies back in the coffin, she closes her eyes and crosses her arms. She has gone back into her sleep-state.)

VAN HELSING

Answer me, my friend! Am I to continue in my work?!

GODALMING

Do as you will, Professor: Do as you will! There can be no horror like this, ever! Anymore!

VAN HELSING

Come now, my friends.

SEWARD

My friend, Arthur, you shall undergo a sore trial. But after, when you will look back, you will see how all this was necessary.

GODALMING

Is this really Lucy's body or only a devil in her shape?

HARKER

Her visage, her appearance is as you had known her in life. But within seethes a vampire, make no mistake.

GODALMING

My true friends, from the bottom of my
broken heart, I thank you all.

MORRIS

Just follow the Professor's orders. And let's
put this thing down like a sick horse.

GODALMING

Tell me what I am to do and I shall not falter.

VAN HELSING

Brave lad. A moment's courage and it is done. This stake must be
driven through her. It will be a fearful ordeal – be not deceived in
that – but it will be only a short time and you will then rejoice more
than your pain was great; from this grim tomb you will emerge as
though you tread on air. But you must not falter when once you have
begun. Only think that we, your true friends, are 'round you, and that
we pray for you all the time.

GODALMING

Go on. Tell me what I am to do.

VAN HELSING

Take this stake in your left hand, ready to place the point over the
heart, her left breast. And take the hammer in your right. Then when
we begin the prayer for the dead, I shall read it. I have here the book,
and the others shall follow – strike in God's name, so that all may
be well with the dead that we love, and assurance that the Un-Dead
shall pass away. Now.

GODALMING

'Tis Lucy as I have seen her in life, with the
face of unequalled sweetness and purity.

VAN HELSING

True, she is now beautiful once more. And now we must stuff her
mouth with garlic and decapitate!

GODALMING

That I cannot do.

MORRIS

Step aside, Art!

*(Music. Morris, Seward, and Harker take turns hammering the stake
into her heart. She reacts with hissing and arms lifting upward. Blood
sprays upward. The men finish the job. Lucy is still, presumably
incapacitated. Music dies out to silence. All is quiet.)*

VAN HELSING

Lord Godalming. Come, it is now safe. You
may take one last look at her.

*(Godalming crosses slowly to the coffin. He peers down at Lucy's
still, lifeless body. A beat. Then in a dramatic and unexpected 'jump-
scare', Lucy screams, bolts upward to grab Godalming. She flails,
writhes, screams more and goes into frightening convulsions. She has
previously been rigged by the actors with a device giving the illusion*

that a stake has run through her. The end of it jutting out her chest, the point clearly visible by several inches from her back.)

VAN HELSING

Arthur, look away! Hold her down, men!

(Music. He begins hammering another stake into her chest. This time one long enough to jut out from the bottom of the coffin, ostensibly pinning her there.)

VAN HELSING

Take her coffin and the remains of her body out of this now sanctified tomb. For there is a terrible task before us! Come!

(They do as instructed. Exeunt.)

[END OF SCENE]

Scene 3

"Baptism of Blood"

[Whitby Asylum]

(Harker and Mina are in the room provided them by Dr. Seward. Though, it isn't what Mina anticipated for their honeymoon suite, she is upbeat and happy that she is with her husband.)

MINA

Who would've thought that upon our wedding, the honeymoon would unfold within the confines of a lunatic asylum.

(They kiss)

HARKER

Indeed, some might argue that it's a fitting commentary on the institution of marriage.

MINA

Oh, Jonathan.

HARKER

Regardless. You are safe with me now.

MINA

Yes, I am… It's a little close in here. Mind if I crack open the window?

(Music)

JONATHAN

Please do. Mina,…. Are you as tired as I am?

MINA

Well, now that you mention it, I do feel rather a bit fatigued.

JONATHAN

It's more than that. I'm almost drowsy.

MINA

Lie down, dear. Rest yourself.

(Music. Jonathan falls into a deep sleep. Dracula mysteriously appears in the room having put Jonathan under and Mina into a trance. He approaches her, reveals his left wrist, cuts it so that it bleeds and places Mina's mouth to the wound. In her trance, she is helpless and ingests his tainted blood. However, he does not have a chance to bite her and ingest her blood completing the communion. For all of a sudden, the male hunters burst into the room, find Jonathan out cold, and Mina within the grasp of the vampire. They raise their crucifixes to him, Van Helsing tosses Holy water upon the beast and Dracula recoils, hissing. Mina breaks free from his hold.)

VAN HELSING

Unhand her, Beast!

GODALMING

Mina, break away!

SEWARD

I'll see to Jonathan.

VAN HELSING

We're here just in time. She has ingested his blood, but he hadn't time to consume hers. The vampire's baptism of blood is not complete. She still has a chance.

SEWARD

He's out cold. I'll use water.

DRACULA

You think to baffle me? You, with your pale faces all in a row. Like sheep in a butcher's. You shall be sorry yet, each one of you! You think you shall leave me without a place to rest; but I have more. My revenge is just begun! I spread it over centuries and time is on my side. Your girls that you all love are mine already; and through them you and others shall yet be mine – my creatures, to do my bidding and to be my jackals when I want to feed!

VAN HELSING

How dare you try to infect yet another with your evil!

DRACULA

Now, *you* shall speak to me? Oh tell me, thou dry men of science, what you see with those oh so bright eyes. *"Omne ignotum pro magnifico!"* Everything that is unknown seems wonderful!

VAN HELSING

I marvel your facility with languages, particularly Latin.

DRACULA

Ah, yes, Latin. It is the language of the Holy, is it not?

VAN HELSING

It is also the language of Satan, himself!

DRACULA

Call me what you will, Van Helsing. But, think you so little of me that you can control my movements? My powers emanate from darkness, a place you fear. I have lived a thousand lives! Think you that it is as simple as six mortals to kill me? You cannot destroy pure evil, for like the energy of the wicked one can neither create or negate, but only observe how it may change form. And in a flash of fire can I vanish, escape, and travel great distances at speeds you cannot imagine! I shall fly from here as a winged devil, where my powers will increase, and my thirst for blood will be quenched. This young girl will forever be under my will! Come after me, if you wish. It is at your peril. When next you see me, it shall be your undoing!

(Dracula vanishes.)

MORRIS

He's gone!

GODALMING

Vanished into the dawn!

SEWARD

Well, at the very least, if he gets caught in the morning's sunlight, he will evaporate into nothing.

VAN HELSING

No, My friend, I'm afraid you're wrong. The toxic relationship between morning's rays and the strigoi has been somewhat exaggerated over the centuries. Though, the light of day may in fact weaken the vampire's powers temporarily, its effects are not altogether deadly to him. It merely lessens his strength, allowing hunters to gain advantage. Come, help Mr. and Mrs. Harker. Bring them with us where they shall be safer. We are protected by the crucifix, the garlic, holy water and scripture! To Doctor Seward's office. I will attempt hypnosis on Mrs. Harker to discover where the vampire has fled!

(Exeunt)

[END OF SCENE]

Scene 4

"Darkness and the Swirling of Water"

[Whitby Asylum]

(Harker goes to one side of the stage. He opens his journal. And begins writing with quill. Van Helsing, Mina, Godalming, Morris and Seward stay gathered in the room. Mina now sitting at the foot of the bed...)

HARKER
(Writing in his journal.)

And so it was, that Professor Van Helsing placed Mina at the foot of the bed in the makeshift 'guest bedroom' at Whitby Asylum. The theory behind the attempt at hypnotism, the Professor told us, was that…

VAN HELSING

…Mina having just experienced a dream-state in which her will is not her own, she will be more susceptible. And since the Count has linked himself to her mind, she may be able to reveal clues about his new whereabouts. So now I shall…

HARKER

…Dangle a gold watch in front of her and swung it carefully from side to side. Mina gazed at him fixedly for a few seconds during which my own heart beat like a trip hammer, for I felt that our crisis was soon at hand. There was a far away look in her eyes, and her voice had a sad dreaminess that was new to me. Van Helsing asked her…

VAN HELSING

Mrs. Harker,… Where are you?

HARKER

She responded that there was…

MINA

…darkness and the swirling of water.

HARKER

She further noted that she could…

MINA

…see a large crate that seems to have
fresh soil scattered about its lid.

HARKER

When asked what she heard, she told us…

MINA

…the creaking of old wood. And then the lapping of water, and waves leaping about.

HARKER

The Professor deduced that the Count had been carried in one of his crates of dirt onto a ship and that the vessel had already embarked on a determined voyage. When we inquired as to which direction, all Mina could say was that she could see…

MINA

…a dark castle in a land beyond the forest.

HARKER

At the which, it was determined that Dracula was on his way back to his native Transylvania to hole up in his castle there. Mina, having a powerful symbiosis with Dracula, was able to intuit the path his wagon-train would be taking. Her clairvoyant premonitions allowed her to draw us a map as to the way he was to go. It was decided, however, that to be on the safe side,…

VAN HELSING

…The best plan of action is not to travel as one caravan,…

SEWARD

…as we would surely be a slow-moving target for marauders.

GODALMING

And should Mrs. Mina's predictions prove faulty?

VAN HELSING

If we divide to conquer, we make it more
difficult for his gypsies to follow us.

MORRIS

We'll stand a better chance of blasting this beast back to Hell.

SEWARD

We travel in pairs.

GODALMING

We rendezvous at the foot of the castle.

HARKER

We realized we had not a moment to lose, that we should pack our
bags and take the fastest train in Dracula's direction we could find,…
The Orient Express!

*(Train whistle. Music. Another train whistle. The individuals each
procure a piece or two of luggage.) (They gather at a designated area
to create the illusion of boarding and sitting in a train.)*

[END OF SCENE]

Scene 5

"The Orient Express"

[Charing Cross Train Station]

*(They gather at a designated area to
establish the boarding platform.)*

VAN HELSING

Then it's all set. Mrs. Harker will travel with me. Jonathan, you will
go with the Lord Godalming.

GODALMING

'Arthur', please. Enough with 'Lord Godalming'. I shall always
remain simply 'Arthur' to my friends.

VAN HELSING

Very well, Jonathan and Arthur travel together.

SEWARD

And Quincey and I will blaze our own path.

VAN HELSING

Goot! You all have your kits, your maps, your separate paths to the
castle. When we arrive, we must organize with haste.

(Train whistle. Enter Conductor played by the
actor who previously played Swales.)

CONDUCTOR

From Charing Cross to Bucharest! ALL ABOARD!!!

(They "board" the train. It is a huddle of the characters sitting on various levels from front being lowest to the last being highest to accommodate the audience being able to see everyone. There is a general, friendly hubbub of ad-libbing as they set down their luggage and find their seats.)

CONDUCTOR

Please have your tickets at the ready.

(The Conductor steps from level to level, down the aisle taking tickets and hole-punching them, then returning each ticket to its respective traveler.)

VAN HELSING

It is important that we all remain awake even throughout our train ride. To sleep is to invite harm come to us at our most vulnerable

GODALMING

I can't nod off anyway. I haven't slept at
all since my poor Lucy died.

MORRIS

Don't you worry 'bout me. I can hold off forty winks, Professor.

SEWARD

I've taken the liberty of administering an injection that should keep me awake for hours to come.

MINA

I'll not sleep, Professor.

HARKER

Nor I. I'll keep wide-eyed and alert, as a sentry to my Mina.

SEWARD

And it appears, we're moving.

VAN HELSING

Let us make an oath. Right here and now. We shall all stay awake and alert. Are we resolved?

(They join hands in the center of the aisle as a show of solidarity.)

ALL

We are resolved.

VAN HELSING

Goot.

(The travelers sit straight-backed, alert, wide-eyed. They look out the windows now and then to be vigilant that they are not being pursued. The following choreography is movement created to convey travel and the passage of time. It is also a bit of needed humor as the vampire hunters were all resolved to stay awake and yet the hypnotic movement of the train seems to have rocked everyone to sleep. It happens in stages throughout the Conductor's announcements.)

<u>CONDUCTOR</u>
All aboard, final call!

(Music and sound of train moving forward on the tracks. The riders convey subtle jostling throughout. Lights fade slowly on the riders down to blackout.)

<u>CONDUCTOR</u>
First stop!

(Lights rise slowly revealing that the travelers' are growing tired. Some with heads heavy, eyelids fluttering, a yawn. Lights fade slowly on the riders down to blackout.)

<u>CONDUCTOR</u>
Second Stop!

(Lights rise slowly revealing that the travelers' are nodding off slightly. It is clear everyone is more drowsy now. Lights fade slowly on the riders down to blackout.)

CONDUCTOR

Third Stop!

(Lights rise slowly revealing that the travelers' are now in varying stages of falling asleep. Lights fade slowly on the riders down to blackout.)

CONDUCTOR

Fourth Stop!

(Lights rise slowly revealing that the travelers' are now fully prostrate in deep sleep. With their bodies all at the lowest possible position, some are propped up against others, some heads back, mouths agape, while others are slumped forward. Waistcoats have become blankets, valises have become pillows. It is a humorous sight.)

CONDUCTOR

Final destination!

(Train whistle. Startled, the travelers wake slowly, stretch, grab their luggage and exit. Music plays into the next scene as the vampire hunters step off the train and exit the scene.)

[END OF SCENE]

Scene 6

"October 31ˢᵗ"

[Aboard the *Czarina Catherine* / Baltic Sea]

(A small corner of the stage. There are sailing ropes, large cloth bags, a lantern or two, crates, and life preservers hung up on the wall.)

<u>HARKER</u>

October 31ˢᵗ, 1893. It is the night prior to all saints. The veil betwixt the living and the dead has now torn at the fabric that holds the metaphysical and the visceral worlds safely disparate. Our train ride from Charing Cross to the ship dock, was, for the most part, uneventful. Arthur and myself are now aboard the *Czarina Catherine*. The Slovaks tell us that a large vessel has passed them. Accounts are that it was traveling at more than usual speed. She had a double crew on board. This was before they came to Fundu. Could not tell us whether the boat turned into the Bistritza or continued on up the Serest. The cold is perhaps beginning to tell upon me. I've entrusted the care of my Mina to the devices of Professor Van Helsing as we are rushing along through the darkness. The cold from the river seems to rise up and strike the ship and mysterious voices of the night surround us. I must now wake my brother in arms; Lord Godalming. We must move to a more secure part of the boat. We seem to be drifting into unknown places and unknown ways; into a whole world of dark and dreadful things. *(Lights fade on scene as Harker gently awakens Lord Godalming. They take up their pallets, blankets, and make-shift pillows, then exit. Lights come up upon another part of the stage representing a clearing. Music carries us through from one scene to the next.)*

[END OF SCENE]

Scene 7

"Precious Cargo"

[Carpathians, Transylvania]

(As music from the previous scene leads in, we see six Slovaks carrying Dracula's empty coffin from a wooded area to the Castle. The carrying is slow, deliberate, formal. Throughout the mysterious underscoring, they ascend the steps, enter the castle, and place the coffin front and center in the middle of the cold, stone floor. The six exit and scatter about into the surrounding woods. Music plays into the next scene.)

[END OF SCENE]

Scene 8

"The Final Conflict"

[Carpathians, Transylvania]

(In music of suspenseful nature, enter the stalking party: Van Helsing, Seward, Harker, Mrs. Harker, Godalming, and Morris. They have made their way to the upper-most peak of Castle Dracula. They enter with lanterns, their 'Vampire kits', and long dowels to be cut into wooden stakes.)

MINA

This is the place! Right here. The villain resides
within the walls of this fortress.

VAN HELSING

A successful rendezvous, wouldn't you say, friends?

(They set up a quick camp in front of the Main entrance, as they prepare to pry their way in.)

GODALMING

Successful, yes, but at the risk of losing one another.

SEWARD

The coffin is within. Through our spyglass we've
seen the gypsies carry the box inside.

HARKER

I'll gather up the cudgels in order that we can carve them down for wooden stakes should we require more. I'll need the saw blade, Quince. Once I've chopped them in thirds we can sharpen the points.

MORRIS

We can use my knife. This thing'll slice a milk pail in half.

(Suddenly, Mina goes into a mystical trance,
wherein she becomes greatly agitated.)

HARKER

Mina, are you all right?

MINA

Something is wrong.

HARKER

Darling, what is it?

(Music. All of a sudden a single gypsy comes out of nowhere and attacks Morris, leaping upon his back. At different points throughout the stage, the gypsies have cleverly hidden, and now make themselves known by the light of their lanterns. Each places his lantern on the ground at his own feet. The hunters stand in a circle facing out. The gypsies close in slowly, then a battle ensues. They fight. Farm tools, homespun implements of torture and lethal weaponry, such as maces, scythes, and clubs are brandished. The battle between the vampire hunters and the gypsies is spectacular, well-choreographed

and exciting. Suddenly, Morris is stabbed by a pitchfork in his abdomen.)

<u>ALL</u>

Quincy! Behind you! He's cut you! Your knife! Kill him! He's got you! Stabbed! Quince!

<u>MORRIS</u>

He only nicked me. I'll be all right.

<u>HARKER</u>

This is our cue, gentlemen. The gypsies
have left an open door. Let's go!

(The vampire hunters are victorious as they overpower the gypsies and run them off one by one. Music continues and the melee moves from the ground area, up to the platform where Dracula's coffin is at center. The hunters then turn their attention to Dracula's coffin. All of a sudden, seemingly from out of smoke, Dracula's three 'brides' in white appear. The three attack the six hunters with surprising vigor and success in holding the interlopers off from nearing the coffin. But, the hunters gain advantage and kill the vampiresses. Van Helsing chops off their heads and hurls them into the ravine below. The hunters go to Dracula's coffin, break open the lid, place a wooden stake at what they believe to be Dracula's body, and drive through with a hammer. But all that puffs upward is a foggy mist. The hunters are taken aback. Dracula appears in an explosion.)

DRACULA

You hunters of wild beasts. Stalkers of the Un-Dead! You thought you saw the Count lying within the box upon the stone. The appearance of soil having fallen off the gypsies' cart had scattered over him. Why he is deathly pale just like a waxen image, and the red eyes glaring with a horrible vindictive look which you know so well. All a stratagem, Fools! Now, see *these* eyes upon the sinking sun. The look of hate in them, now turning to triumph! For the Castle Dracula now stands out against a red sky and every stone of its broken battlements articulated within the light of the setting sun. My powers rise! It shall be fully dark soon. And then my strength shall increase a hundred fold! Your corpses, should you escape the curse of my blood shall soon lie among the rubble of this fortress for eternity!

HARKER

Like you, so too have I long awaited this day. And now begins *my* work. The butcher's work! Had I not been unnerved by thoughts of other dead, and of the living over whom hang such a pall of fear, I might not have gone on. God be thanked my nerve, *our* nerves do stand. Shall I go further with my butchery? The horrid screeching as the stake drives home; the plunging into your writhing form, and your lips of bloody foam as we cast you forever to the Hell from whence you were spawned?

DRACULA

You should have fled in terror and left your work undone. But it is over! Come, join us in our immortality. Do you not want to live forever? I alone possess the ultimate power to either destroy each and every one of you, or grant you eternal life, forever stalking the earth in darkness. The choice is yours. Insufferable torture, exquisite pain and your cries for mercy, shall they go unheard? Is that how you wish to die? A miserable death at my hands? Or join my congregation, and learn what we have learned. The blood is the life!

HARKER

We have forced our way to your lair. We are Hell-bent on finishing our task, before the sun sets completely. Neither the pointed weapons leveled by the gypsies in front, nor the howling of the wolves behind, will avert our cause. I've grown weary of waiting. It is time now. Words fail me!

DRACULA

Perhaps your beautiful wife will prove less tongue-tied.

HARKER

MINA!!! NO!!!

(Mina begins to go to Dracula in her spell. The men make their move and attack Dracula with a vengeance. The vampire is trapped and Harker drives a stake straight through his heart.

VAN HELSING

Hold him, John! It is not enough to drive the stake through his heart. A long-blade through his side must intersect with the stake and form a cross.

SEWARD

Quincey, your hunting knife!

GODALMING

I've got him, now Quincey! Stab him! Form the cross!

(Morris stabs Dracula through his side presumably creating a 'cross' in the center of the vampire's heart. Dracula, in great pain evaporates into dust. In music, Morris turns his side towards the audience, places his fingers at the wound on his side and pulls back with a handful of flowing blood. He falls. Seward runs to him.)

SEWARD

Mr. Morris! Quincy! *(Seward examines the wound.)* The gypsy's pitchfork has gone straight through! His vital organs have been punctured. There's too much bleeding. We cannot save him.

MORRIS

No, it's all right. Leave me. Leave me. I'm only too happy to have been of any service. Oh, God! It was worth this to die. Now God be thanked that all has not been in vain. See! Look at your wife! The snow is not more stainless than Ms. Mina's forehead. The curse has passed away! No, no, leave me, friends to die alone. Afford me, just that much dignity.

VAN HELSING

Let him go, Arthur. Leave him to his privacy.

HARKER

May you have eternal peace, brave friend.

(As music underscores, Quincey Morris dies. His cohorts all go into a hard freeze, a beautiful and telling tableau. Van Helsing breaks from the tableau and crosses downstage to address the audience. Music continues to underscore the following.)

VAN HELSING

And to our bitter grief, with a smile and silence, he died, a gallant gentleman. But, I was not fully relieved after our final conflict. For it seems that I alone realized something my friends had not. Quincy Morris stabbed Dracula through the heart with a single huntsman's knife. In order to truly destroy the vampire, however, there needed to have been a second weapon thrust into the monster's side, creating a cross with both blades. Or as is more commonly done, a wooden stake through the heart would fell the creature. In our haste to dispatch the fiend, no stakes were used. It was Mr. Morris' hunting knife which pierced the heart and appeared to reduce the vampire king to dust. I fear that like purity and goodness, the wicked cannot be fully destroyed, but only held at bay. For a time. *(The upper door of Dracula's chamber slowly creeks open on its own accord. A flood of blood-red light glows out from the open door.)* Heaven forbid it shall one day rise like the phoenix in the hollow boom of a thunderclap! May this evil remain averted for eons we pray, throughout vast oceans of time. For our part? We all went through the flames. And the happiness of some of us, since then is, we think, well worth the pain we endured.

(The four surviving members of the stalking party come out of their freeze. Van Helsing joins them. Gypsies from the nearby village enter gradually, slowly. They are robed and hooded gypsy women with covered faces. They also enter one by one each holding a beautiful, lit candelabra. Quincy's body is taken up respectfully by Harker, Van Helsing, Godalming, and Mrs. Harker. Slowly, gradually, all have gathered and formed a line until it appears that twenty or so are all exiting in a solemn procession. We are left with the powerful image of a host of humanity, seeing their way through the darkness with glowing candelabras, held high, flickering, twinkling in the moonless sky. The procession continues until all have exited and the last flame is seen gradually disappearing into the night. Music comes to a grand end. Fade to black.)

END OF PLAY

CHRISTOFER COOK (Playwright) holds an MFA from the Theatre Conservatory of Roosevelt University in Chicago, an MA from South University, and a BA from Winthrop College. In 2014 his play, Washington Irving's *The Legend of Sleepy Hollow*, made its European premiere in Kent, England. His play adaptations include *DRACULA of Transylvania, Frankenstein's Creature, A Night of the Living Dead, Phantom of the Opera* and *The Tell-Tale Heart*. Cook is the author of The Vampire Diaries; *'Nosferatu Trilogy'*, available via Amazon Kindle. He is a member of the Dramatist's Guild of America, the Horror Writer's Association, The Dark Fiction Guild, and the Dracula Society.

DACRE STOKER (Script Advisor) is the great grand nephew of Bram Stoker and the bestselling co-author of *Dracula the Undead* (Dutton, 2009), the official Stoker family endorsed sequel to *Dracula*. Dacre is also the co- editor (with Elizabeth Miller) of *The Lost Journal of Bram Stoker: The Dublin Years* (Robson Press, 2012). Dacre has consulted and appeared in recent film documentaries about vampires in literature and popular culture. He currently hosts tours to Transylvania exploring both the life and times of the historic Vlad Dracula III and the locations where Bram Stoker set his famous novel. He currently lives in Aiken, SC with his wife Jenne. They manage the Bram Stoker Estate.

Printed in the United States
By Bookmasters